THE PECULIARITIES OF YEARNING

Stephanie Carty is a writer, trainer and NHS Consultant Clinical Psychologist in the UK. Her short fiction has been shortlisted and placed in numerous competitions including Bristol Short Story Prize, Aesthetica Creative Writing Award, Caterpillar Story for Children Prize, Bath Flash Fiction Award and Bridport Prize. Her novella-in-flash, *Three Sisters of Stone*, won Best Novella at the 2019 Saboteur Awards.

ALSO BY STEPHANIE CARTY

Three Sisters of Stone

Inside Fictional Minds: Tips from psychology for creating characters

The Peculiarities of Yearning

Stephanie Carty

To
Steve,
Thanks for all your
support along this
writing road,
Stephanie

REFLEX PRESS

First published as a collection in 2022 by Reflex Press
Abingdon, Oxfordshire, OX14 3SY
www.reflex.press

A CIP catalogue record of this book is
available from the British Library.

ISBN: 978-1-914114-04-5

1 3 5 7 9 10 8 6 4 2

Printed and bound in Great Britain by
Imprint Digital, Upton Pyne, Exeter

Cover image by Louise Ryder Hall

www.reflex.press/the-peculiarities-of-yearning/

CONTENTS

Rules of the High Wire

Don't look down. Focus only on your feet. Yes, it is more challenging in high heels and the restrictions of a silk dress. Exhale.

You catch sight of movement beneath you. Free runners; barefoot and shameless. They act as if a straight line doesn't give direction, backing up on themselves to chatter. Feel nothing towards them; they make their own mistakes.

Face forward. Try not to notice how the clouds around you form themselves into faces. They are merely raindrops clutching together before a storm. Up ahead, the birds gather. They swoop and circle as one. Do not take the shapes they draw in the sky as a message to you.

Carry that burden on your back as if it's weightless. Straighten up, don't show weakness. Counter the weight with a light smile, nothing too showy.

As the skies darken for another long night, keep onwards. Walk the wire that you know is beneath your feet. Don't become mesmerised by distractions of starlight and the calls of night creatures. They have no purpose, no journey, no glory to come.

Do not think about what happens when you reach the end of the line.

Born from Red

The school is on lockdown for a random colour check, and I hear whispers that Leila has climbed out of the bathroom window, taking her painted toenails to safety. The rule is absolute: we must not see red. We line up in rows of cream and grey with our shirt sleeves rolled up. Our skirts touch our knees, showing pimply skin where the hairs have been waxed as we are not permitted blades. Any scratch or cut must be covered with a bandage. It is safer to stay at home until your body is back the way it's intended – without the colour of the devil.

A nurse checks that all girls are taking their medication – no menstruation is allowed, of course, as that is the fiercest red there is. There was a girl in the year above me who vomited out her meds, or forgot them, or had a dark desire to see her own blood. She was dismissed that day. We had to hang our heads and stare at the floor as she was escorted out. I wriggled my toes to wave goodbye, but the rigid leather of my shoes hid my cowardly act.

After the checks, there is shared relief that shows itself in skittishness and rumours. It's the one afternoon of the term when the male instructors lean back in their chairs and permit us to speak to each other in class. I wonder at their intentions. The best way to keep control is to let our mouths spread stories and blame. My classmates' tongues click away at her name – Leila, Leila, Leila. I sit straight-backed and count with each breath to tame my heartbeats. Even as I recite poetry in my head, I see the image of my blood-red heart beating her name, sending the urge to run down into my legs. I am grateful that it's Friday and I have two days of freedom to find her. She will not return to class on Monday.

Once the sun is high up above us, I tell Dad I have botany specimens to collect and will be back by supper time. He is gluing small parts onto a ship that looks no different to any of the others he has made. He glances up from his handiwork to me, and – although I squeezed my hands into a fist in preparation – I can't help but look away from the scarlet filaments that streak his eyes. These rivulets of red tell a story of lonely nights with only a vodka bottle to hold. My mother chose not to move to the safety of this village before I even started school. We do not speak of her. I hear the pulsing blood in my ears that keeps me alive while threatening to ruin me.

'No sharps, stay clean, Anna,' he says and wraps some bread in cloth for me to take. I hold my breath as I kiss the top of his head to stop him inhaling my intentions.

I take the path that leads from the back of our row of cottages towards the woods. The bluebells that kissed these grounds have already gone for another year. I walk fast enough to ache the back of my legs and burn my chest. Stillness or speed, nothing in-between. The curves of the path are as familiar as those of my signature. I once tried to walk the length with my eyes closed, certain that I could navigate the route. The elation of the first twenty yards was smashed as I tripped over and landed on my hands. Criss-cross lines in the forbidden colour kept me off school for a week and caused me such shame I stayed in bed with the drapes drawn to dull the hue.

I settle by the stream on a welcoming bank of grass to wait for her. This is our spot. She showed me how to fish with just a stick and fast hands. Leila wears no sun cream or hat, so her skin is older than her years, brown and rich. I am slathered in lotion to ensure that no patches of red appear on my shoulder blades or across my nose. We are taught that lips are naturally pink, but Leila's are as red as they are plump. She laughed when I told her this, curling my hair behind my ear. She told me of food from her grandmother's farm hidden high in the hills: the luscious tomatoes and sweet dripping apples, the opposite of green.

I doze in the warmth, the sunlight drifting through the mesh of my hat.

Leila speaks my name and tickles the back of my hand with a fern. My words won't come. She flings off her shoes and wobbles on one foot to show me her toenails. The rumours were true – they are painted a red so shiny that I squint.

'I've got something for us to try, if you like.' Leila talks through her hands, which curl around each word and continue talking after her mouth stops. Sometimes they talk instead of her lips, like the time she pulled me to the roadside to look at the crushed bloodied carcass of a deer. She uncurls her hand and shows me little red and white mushrooms. I clench my teeth. Then nod.

We climb a little further into the trees for cover. Leila doesn't get out of breath like I do. She knows facts that aren't in any book that we are allowed. I don't ask her how she knows. She tells me that these are toadstools, like in the fairy tales. I recall them being dusky pink and pure white. Leila laughs with her head tipped back, the length of her neck on view.

'Listen, Anna, you don't have to take them with me. They could make us pretty sick. But before they do, they'll show us a different world.' She is glowing. I tell myself that my nausea is excitement. My last weekend with Leila. I catch myself digging my nails into my palms and stop before any marks are made.

Leila arranges the toadstools on a piece of bark and chops them with a knife she pulls from her pocket. I long to run my finger along its edge. We chew the foamy pieces and sip river water from a flask, then we share my bread. Leila tells me she is going to go and work on her grandmother's farm, just outside the limits of the village. They keep animals I've never been near. My head starts to whirl as she tells me about lambs getting stuck in their mothers and pigs that reject their young. She hasn't learnt this only from letters sneaked in through the delivery boy – she must have been out there, in the world we were born into. The elbow I'm leaning on collapses under me, so I lie flat on the grass hearing the thud of the land. Leila's legs shake until she drops down to the ground near me and lies down. I feel the sting of bile at the back of my throat.

'Don't fight it, Anna, let it show you things. I'm right here.'

She grabs my hand, and the trees bend towards me as if to hold us together. I can't tell if it's the trees spinning around and around or us. Or have we only just noticed that the world is turning? The grass underneath my body shoots up around us and springs into flowers larger than my head. Ripples run up and down my body as if I'm lying on the riverbed.

I float up above the forest floor, higher and higher. Our village of green fields, pink flowers and white houses. There is the school, glowing so brightly I squeeze my eyes for protection. Then I dive down, down towards the ground, which opens beneath me. I land in a labyrinth of tunnels and press my back against hot, earthy walls. Rivers of red run under the school, flowing outwards to escape to the forest. Swimming in the claret waters are beautiful women with their swollen pregnant forms. They turn to float on their backs, smiling and singing to their unborn. Standing waist-high in the lapping water, a couple intertwine while kissing – their hands grip and swirl across each other. I look more closely at the liquid. In place of disgust, I feel peace and passion and what it is to be a woman. We were all born from red.

My body rises and floats easily out of the tunnels as my eyes linger on the scene I wish to stay in. Everything turns pure white as I return to my breathing body. The lulling waves change to stormy seas as I turn to my side to retch again and again. Sweat pours from the back of my neck as I free my stomach of all its bitterness.

My limbs start to obey my commands. The trees are back in their place, nothing but tall conifers swaying in the wind, oblivious to us. I turn to Leila and smile. She squeezes my hand in hers. Then I remember. My mother's hand encasing mine as she sang sweet melodies. My father screaming that her summer dress showed her off like a whore. The smash of his bottle. Red flowing down her arm with shards of glass between us. Her shouting at me to keep away, to go to my room and stay under the covers. And later, again and again, Dad on his knees, rocking forward and back as he prayed. Mumbling words through liquor-warmed lips, begging the Lord to keep us safe from the devil that lives in all women.

The danger is not out there, beyond the pastel safety of our village limits. It is not inside me. It is not a colour. I stand up and scan the higher land beyond the fencing. Paths curve their way up through the sloping fields – invitations in a thousand directions. One of them leads to my mother.

Leila still holds my hand as we make our way along an overgrown path towards the outskirts of the village. Our embracing fingers do the work of words. As the sun sets, the pink and white of the sky merge at the horizon into a deep red.

Aspects of My Father

After my father died, Mother and I had his body preserved to keep him around the house. As part of his head was sprayed over the back of the garage, we had the option to replace it. We selected four heads from a catalogue for the unexpectedly widowed. The waxy skin was malleable. I smoothed his brow of judgment and pinched laughter lines around his mouth. At last, I could make my father smile.

My favourite replacement head looked like a cartoon therapist with an inquisitive moustache. At first, it seemed strange to call him Father. But the gin unfurled my tongue, and I whispered truths of regret into his deaf ear.

The middle-aged head with freckled cheeks advised me to stop chewing gum all day so that I could smell the world around me again, connect with the concoctions in the air. A younger head with ginger flecks in his beard sighed and said he wanted me to remember what it felt like to be held. And the handsome head with cheekbones like Paul Newman ordered me in a firm but fair way to act like the thirty-two-year-old I was and get out in the world.

I left my mother's house for the first time since my divorce. When I returned late, I still smelt the tang of life from the city on my coat. I'd inhaled hope amongst the cigarette smoke and perfumed necks. I peered through the crack of Mother's door. She lay cradled in arms that once belonged to my father. In the gloom, I could not make out which head rested against hers.

I packed my bags with clothes of every colour except black. On the way to the front door, I grabbed Father's huge umbrella to shelter me from the sobbing skies.

Waking Beauty

Just as my legs weakened underneath skirts of linen and lace, I caught sight of Papa's painting from his travels of that exquisite beast, the wolf. It stared into the distance as if it could see ahead to that which now descended on us. From the kitchens escaped the sighs and exclamations of the staff, as they felt the oncoming faint and fell to sleep right where they were. As my eyes closed, I wondered what the gentlemen of the house would make upon waking to find a girl asleep amongst the leather and musk of the library room.

I feel her presence before she even touches me. Stuck fast between a dream world and that which I left a long time ago, my body does not obey my will. Then her breath as she pants inquisitively. A lick from her tongue against my face warms a part of me that had forgotten how to move. Curled on the floor, I start to unwind my stiff body. As my eyelids flutter back to life, she pads towards the window and leaps.

The solemn silence of the house speaks to me of my family's fate. They sleep still. Mama perhaps nestled in her chamber draped in dreams and silk, Papa folded forward over his plans for war. Shall I fall back to the peace of sleep, never woman nor wife?

My clothing pulls me down as the earth pulls rain. I untie my dress. As it drops away, I find my breath, my body. Light as a fern. Trees have stretched their arms into our slumbering house. The finger of a branch beckons me outdoors. I roll down my stockings and free my feet from their gaol. Unpinning my hair, I shake it over my shoulders, the touch of which causes my skin to dance and pimple. There are no ladies to watch over me, an unbetrothed young lady. I sigh out my name and leave it behind in the cobwebs.

I follow my visitor's path through the window. My breath leaves a trail of white shadow in the night. Saliva gathers in a pool within my mouth. As I start to run, it drips down over my teeth and runs down my chin. I catch a flash of movement and freeze. A rabbit. Not hanging upside down in the kitchens but sniffing and shuffling right there. My chest pounds a rhythm of not-now-not-now, but I feel the ache of hunger.

Then I become the heartbeat, the clatter of branch against branch, the swirl of searching wind feeling its way between the trees to bend the smallest blade of grass as I exhale. I am the rich dark soil, crawling with opportunity and death. I am the yellow moonlight dripping in pools of storm water. I am the broken colours of the sun, the ever-moving yet still forest of the night. The silent damage, the hidden hunter and the always-will-be.

Quads

Mothering multiples is tough. No room to breathe.

The Tiny Twins never got as far as having their own names. Forever nine weeks gestation, their curled bodies hover in the corner. Little not-quite-legs tucked underneath contentedly. They don't suffer. But when the house is still, I hear them whisper, 'Why me? Why me?'. I have no answer to why those two, not their siblings. Two out of four. We had to make room, play the odds. The doctor said they were too young to feel, would be absorbed by my body while the other two thrived. I told no one on the ward that when I came round from the drugs and dissociation, the Twins floated beside me. No judgement, just constant confusion: *why, why, why?*

When living people talked at me – assessed, measured, reassured – all my mouth did was turn upwards. I listened for what the remaining babies said, but they spoke only through movement under my skin. Were they fighting to get out to be with their siblings? Or was this a battle to the death which only one would survive?

In the incubators, the Twins' big sisters Grace and Una had looked so similar. Grace's lungs weren't ready. Her furry limbs reached out, but I couldn't get to her through the Perspex and terror. We received cards decorated with flowers and Jesus before the teddy bears of congratulations had been put away.

While I'm entranced by the Twins' bobbing movements like fish in a tank, Grace throws something heavy above my ear. I drop to my knees, holding my head in my hands. She's a couple of feet above me, her waking shrieks adding to the pressure in my skull. Without looking, I know her tiny arms are outstretched. Her yearning burns me. She yanks at the cord that connects us to gain my attention. My womb lurches with the pull. But we both know – however hard I try to reach up – she will always float higher. I climbed up onto the roof one time. Grace remained two feet above me, straining. The paramedics didn't understand.

Through the gloopy fog of sleep deprivation, I pull out the tune but not the words to songs Grace likes. She starts to settle, releases the tension on the cord so I don't throw up this time. There are three more hours before Rob will be home. How many loops of the lullabies will that take? One hundred? One thousand? Numbers don't make sense anymore. I sing songs about special girls, about babies sleeping, about mummy's love. I never sing *Rock-A-Bye Baby*.

My body aches from the pull of the cord. Rob says I should eat more, but it's cruel to show the children things they can't join in with. All three sway to the music. Two more hours. They quieten when their father is home, no need to worry him. None of us liked that stay at St Jude's, where they dosed me with so many medications my little ones were left to fend for themselves, drifting in silence.

I lean against the wall and hum. Muffled sounds from a television travel from the room below me. Una is probably getting herself a bite to eat while watching cartoons. Such a good girl, no trouble at all.

The Fairground

Intoxicating lights lure me, night-bitten. Not a place for good girls, not a place for fresh flesh. But the strongman beckons with the bass of a whale. My thighs pulsate. He feeds me cotton candy till my molars are glued into a forever smile. He likes it that way. I shoot, shoot, shoot at the passing ducks, but all my luck left. The strongman smashes them down in one swoop, reaching over to hand me a goldfish in a bag. That makes three of us now. I watch the trapped fish swim in a loop as if it might end up somewhere different. Nausea surges. On the merry-go-round, I think I pass my father, smoking his pipe, hands behind his back. When I come around once more, he has vanished. Or never was. People scream as they whoosh down the rollercoaster, but only because they know they are safe. I stay silent. In the hall of mirrors, he holds my waist as I see all versions of him: charming, snarling, violent, sorry. The band around my wrist cuts into me. But I have paid my fee, so I will stay.

The Science of Self

Lana traps her blood sample between two rectangles of glass and watches as little fingers of red stretch outwards for freedom. She guessed there may be Viking DNA inside her. That would explain the pull of the sea, the shield she carries inside, the craving to burn it all to the ground. The slides are sucked into a machine that hums its calculations. She yanks the results out.

TOP LOCATION MATCHES: SMALL SPACES; ENTANGLED DREAMS; IN-BETWEEN.

Perhaps she selected the wrong mode. Lana folds the paper precisely and turns its judgement into a small boat that would never last on the open seas.

A pipette shows Lana's urine as orange as the low sun. She's been too distracted lately to bother with basics like hydration. Or touch. It all seems so indulgent. She lets one drop fall onto the test card. An underactive gland or hopeless hormone could be remedied swiftly enough. The electronic result beeps.

NOT PREGNANT. YOU SHOULD HAVE KEPT IT WHEN YOU HAD THE CHANCE.

Lana crosses her legs. There are multivitamins at the back of the kitchen cupboard. She could take those if she summoned enough saliva.

Next, Lana holds her palm against the computer screen. The gel-like surface gives way a little, like her memory foam mattress that carries the indentations of last decade's dreams. The computer sighs as it reads her fingerprints. She squints at the results.

82% PROBABILITY: WANTED FOR CRIMES AT 42 HAYLAND GROVE.

That's her address. Nothing bad has happened there. Not to someone else, anyway. She washes her hands at the basin, scrubbing those finger-tip ridges that mean she can't be anybody else.

For the final task, Lana yanks a hair from its root. It comes out with a satisfying jolt of near pain. She submerges it in solution. A peculiar word because there doesn't appear to be one. No solutions, no answers, no certainty. She's no closer to knowing what she is made of. The computer dashboard flashes.

A WOMAN OF NO SUBSTANCE.

She'd laugh if she could unlock her jaw.

'Nothing lost, nothing gained,' she tells her toes, but her innards disagree. Lana runs her finger along the smooth, sleek edges of the computer monitor. It maintains its sheen and optimum temperature throughout. Her shirt feels damp against her skin, suddenly too constricting.

PRINT FINAL RESULTS?

Exit or enter. Exit. Enter. Exit. Enter. Lana closes her eyes and lets her thumb decide with a click.

The 3D printer vibrates so much the floor shakes, sending waves of ones and zeros up her legs. The door is one metre away if she chooses not to stay for the outcome. But the sum of the parts could be greater than the whole.

Lana freezes as if breathing were optional. Stretching out of the printer one limb at a time is another Lana. She looks tired and thin, too. But she smiles in a way that doesn't hurt. The New Lana opens her arms out and waits.

Games O'Clock

I'm not just good at games, I'm good at knowing what time to play the right one. I can teach you all about it.

It's Morning o'clock. There's no battery in the clock but I can tell cos the lorries are shaking my bedroom door. The curtains are all shiny from the sun. It is best to keep all the curtains shut when mummy is out because people can't see in but you can still use your sneaky eye to see out just in case of social workers who we call child-catchers which sounds scary but just laugh cos it's funny really. The cat is meowing for the lady next door to open up. She won't be up until Fag Time in the back yard. He will stop meowing soon and just go and find something fun to do by himself cos that is better than waiting and crying. Fag Time is not for ages but is sooner than mummy will get home. That might be Soaps o'clock cos she does not like to miss the telly. It's time for the Criss Cross game, where I pretend to be a grown up and get ready all by myself.

You might be looking at my nightie right now and thinking that's not even a nightie what a silly girl. Well it is called a night shirt and it smelt of nana when I found it in the cupboard but now it mostly smells of my feet and shake n vac which is flowery talc for your carpet if it smells a bit of wee (by accident). The hoover is broke so I just do the Swish Swash game with my shoes and the talc goes in and everything smells better, for a bit anyway.

So we need to go downstairs and get breakfast. It's not scary in the day time so don't worry. Keep your shoes on though. I will show you how to do the Squeaky Stair game on the way down – don't tread on the ones that make a noise. This is just a practice game, in case you ever need to go on the stairs when mummy is poorly or there is a visitor in her bedroom. I'm going to have coco crisps which I don't even need to find a bowl for cos if you lick your tongue into the box they all stick on so it doesn't matter that there's no milk. I like to lick my breakfast in the telly room. Do you know some people don't like the adverts but they're my favourite and if you wiggle your fingers while you watch them it's a bit like you've really got those toys just for yourself. Then we can watch as much telly as we want.

~

Next door's gate is squeaking open for Fag Time which comes with cough, cough, cough which sounds a bit like mummy being sick if she has not had her medicine. That makes me think of my Barbie box cos they are all as skinny as mummy so I will show you all my dolls and we can play Fashion Show. The toes and fingers are chewed up cos you have to stop sucking your thumb when you're a big girl and you have to find something else to do with your mouth. Barbie's hair is a bit messy cos I don't know how you do plaits so I just twist it round and round but it won't stay and it all twirls back which makes me cross cos I want her to stay pretty and just right. I like all her different clothes. I bet my mummy would look lovely in princess dresses instead of tights with holes and skirts that nana said must have shrunk in the wash.

I can do your make-up if you want. I lost the little brushes but I can use my fingers, see. We can pretend there's sparkles. It is important to make your eyes look pretty. The black bit in the middle of your eye is where the light goes in so you can see. Sometimes mummy's black bits go teeny and so maybe she can't see me and that's why she just stares at the wall until she falls asleep.

Me and mummy play games together I can teach you about. One is called Hungry Pockets. You wear a coat with lots of pockets and zips. Then you go in the shop and see if you can put things in your pocket but you can't laugh or get caught. Mummy is good at this but her pockets sometimes eat boring things like cheese. Don't you try it in our house though cos I know where everything should be even if it looks a mess to you.

~

My tummy tells me it's Lunch o'clock. I have a trick to show you. First you take the plastic off the cheese, see it looks like just one square? Now I fold it this way, then across again, and I have made four squares of cheese instead! We can have this with four crackers and there won't even be any pudding space left.

I like to wobble on these big stools in the kitchen and sniff next door's fag smoke cos it reminds me of nana. She put those photos on the fridge of my brothers. Little Teddy has a new mummy now. Bobby lives with his dad who is not the same dad as my dad. I'm not sure why he didn't want me to live with him too cos I could have done all the jobs for him. I think it might be because Bobby and his dad have blonde hair the same as each other but I have brown like mummy. Little Teddy's hair and legs probably don't match his new mummy and daddy's. You might not know, but I'm playing the Not Bothered game right now.

~

This box under the stairs is very heavy but I can move it with my feet if I lie down. It's got loads of train track that Bobby used to play with when he still visited. We can make a massive track down the hall and into the telly room.

But uh-oh did you hear that? Don't move. It's the front door.

Now we have to play Statues cos that is not mum who has forgotten her key – she would not knock, knock, knock like that but would call me through the letter box. Don't move even if you need a wee or you really want to squeeze your eyes through the curtains to see if it's a child-catcher. You have to sing one hundred green bottles in your head and start again if you hear any more knocks or talking.

I'm really good at Statues. It's a secret, but I don't even sing one hundred green bottles in my head anymore. I just close my eyes and think about nice things like the time nana and Bobby and me and mum went for a picnic. I couldn't get the straw in my juice which was a treat, so nana came and squeezed it too hard and it went all over her, and mummy laughed so much she said a bit of wee came out.

~

It's alright to go back to the telly room now. I will put mummy's best CD on which is Madonna and I will show you how me and mummy do the Vogue Game when she is not tired or poorly or working all night. You have to think of new moves when it's your turn don't just copy me. Mummy can be very funny when she is happy and drinks wine and she lets me stay up as late as I want so I can watch her. Mummy says she loves me fiercely which sounds like angry but means no one will ever take me away. She gets tired quick cos her skin is tight on her bones and she doesn't like dinners any more. But let's have a disco now cos when mummy gets home she will need to go to bed and we will have to play Fingers on Lips.

~

Nana's china dogs are rattling on the shelves. She had loads, even ones that are ugly and broken but she loved them cos they were hers. The cars are all driving back from work so it's Dinner o'clock. We don't have a car but if we did I would have one that the roof comes off and I would let mine and mummy's brown hair blow in the wind while we laugh and drive to find the sea. I've got a shell in my bedroom that nana said sounds like the sea. I will go to the sea when I'm grown up. I will take mummy and Bobby and I will find Teddy who won't be little anymore. We can have snacks and mummy will have new batteries which means she won't have medicine that makes her sleep all the time. You can come if you want.

I'm going to have two bags of crisps for dinner – prawn cocktail and salt and vinegar. Me and mummy have a joke that this is called Fish and Chips. You might not want to sit next to me cos it's a bit stinky. If you are missing your own house and your family, you can borrow my marbles. Put two in your hand and make them go around and around all cold and glassy. Or under the stairs I have some fuzzy felt animal shapes which are good for rubbing if your tummy misses someone. I think I'm going to do some exercises like this handstand so that my muscles are strong if I need to fight a visitor or get away from a child catcher or pinch someone under the table at school who says something horrible about mummy.

~

It's Soaps o'clock but mummy isn't home. You can stay a bit more if you like. I think I will watch the telly so I can tell mummy what happened. You can go upstairs and find mummy's Don't Go In drawers. They are Top Secret but I won't tell. If mummy found out you could say oh no I got mixed up. Me and mummy used to play a game in the One Pound Shop where we ask the lady 'How much is this?' as many times as we could without laughing or being chucked out of the shop. If you ever get in trouble, just pretend you didn't know the rules and then have a cry.

~

I'm going to put my nightie back on for Late o'clock. While I get ready you can borrow my princess diary that has a real lock on it. I can't find the key but I think it's still secret. If you have any feelings, you can write them in there and then they are not stuck in your tummy. Nana taught me that. I only write my made-up words, just in case anyone finds it. You won't hear me going to bed cos I'm going to practise the Squeaky Stair game. I'm sure mummy will come back next Soap o'clock. You probably just want to go home now. That's fine. But if you want, you could stay and sleep on the sofa. You could practise the Not Bothered game. And maybe you could teach me some of your games tomorrow?

A Hunger That Can't Be Undone

The sandwiches are cut into tiny triangles as if for children, but there are no children left. Little sausages nestle together on bone china plates. Pastries too beautiful to crush lie untouched. Mothers' cheekbones hover under hollowed eyes as we look anywhere but at each other. Loss burns under my ribs. I smooth out a napkin and lay a sharp knife to rest within it before burying it in my handbag.

Our torsos are encased in black. Necks glimmer with heavy gold to weigh us down, to stop us floating right through the open window, up and up to join our little ones. In the far corner of the school hall, rows of photographs fill a table of purple velvet. Their rigid faces match our own. My eyes retreat from the obscenity of colour in the bouquets.

Numbness is worse than pain. If I could reach into the past, I'd lay my hand against the hot, broken metal. I'd walk into the flames as they licked the coach door, pushing our babies back to the smoke. I'd inhale with such violence there would be no smoke left to smother the innocents. I pull at my necklace and gasp at air as thick as soup. Reaching into my hair, I dig sharp nails into my scalp to return to now. To a body and heartbeat that I don't deserve. I grip the arm of a chair.

One mother rubs a palm over her full womb in never-ending circles. Her lips remember how to smile. Blood pulses morse code messages into my ears from my empty insides. I snatch up fistfuls of food and thrust them into my mouth, leaving no room to shout out. Then I wrap my fingers around the knife handle in my bag and squeeze until my fist tremors.

Geology of a Girl

Ella kept one pebble in her pocket and rubbed it down to sand, running the grains through her fingers. Stones sneaked in through holes in her shoes. Her legs turned to rock. She leant against the sisterhood of brick on the playground and watched girls skip together like lambs. A boulder weighed heavy in her stomach. She curled forwards by habit. Her head filled with the detritus of life.

A new girl started school in May with fire in her eyes. She whispered to Ella with aniseed breath, *'Lava is liquid rock,'* then took her hand and ran.

Listening to the Library

Thousands of paper friends surround me: they are trying to tell me something. As I walk along aisles of the library, I inspect each book that is slightly out of line. I let it fall open, jot down whichever word calls to me into a leather-bound notebook that before today seemed too precious to suffer my gangly writing. I gifted it to myself on my thirtieth birthday, with no wife to stroke the emerging grey hairs in my beard, no children to bounce around me with cake-coated smiles.

At the non-fiction shelves, I place my notebook onto the ground. These hard-backed books have waited patiently for attention. I caress their spines. My fingertips soak up each letter in turn. My skin tingles with the possibility of opening the door to an answer.

This afternoon, a young woman with wavy hair to her waist and Neptune eyes hesitated by the scanner. She held 'Birds of the World' in a delicate hand, the tip of each nail painted white. Rather than keep my eyes down, I pointed to the Eastern Bluebird with its delicate features and cobalt plumage.

'This is you,' I said.

She leant over the page as I pushed my toes into the carpet.

'Thank you,' she replied.

I retreated before anything could undo the spell, left my bluebird to fly away.

As a child, I'd crafted words into my own code in notebooks. An alphabet of life: ache, bruise, crush, demon, escape, fly, gone. 'Some boys are born bad,' they'd said. 'You can't escape what you're made of.' I pushed so much away that in the end, no more pushing was needed. Numbness became my nest.

It's time to listen to the library. Out of my pores float the words I absorbed. Messages gather from Eastern Studies, Ornithology, Anatomy, Current Affairs. They whoosh above me into order.

Concentrate your mind on the present moment. Freedom of flight beckons through lightweight bones and strength. Listen closely for murmurs from the heart. The time is now.

These phrases hang in the air, glowing like fairy lights. Through an arched window, the world waits patiently for the morning, meaning me no harm.

I feel a shift inside. The letters of my nature no longer sentence me. My DNA dances, re-arranged.

Stasis

The Baby Stasis Machine arrived just two weeks after I first discussed the idea with an equally tired friend. I found the box on our front porch, a thoughtful gift. It was to be used for short bursts – maybe fifteen minutes – to pause a child and make life manageable. Just enough time for a quick shower, or to prepare food, or to cry under the duvet at the monotony of life. I bought shower mousse that covered my distended skin in thick white foam, hiding the scar and sagging skin. Before I could rinse it all away, the machine beeped, and baby started to cry. It was simply not long enough.

I tried a double cycle. Thirty whole minutes. My blow-dried hair bounced like in a commercial. My socks matched. I realised that baby's big sister had such supple joints she could fold herself into the machine. While baby napped, I paused my toddler and remembered how great it felt to sing a song that didn't rhyme, to eat cake without crouching in the corner, to not lock the bathroom door.

My husband commented on my improved mood, nodded his approval when I lied that I was eating more nuts and drinking only boiled water. Husbands hear what they want to hear. *There is a wide range of normal development in babies,* I told him, *no need to call it 'delay'*. Baby would make up for lost time spent in stasis, eventually.

When had I ever put my own needs first? On the airplane that brought us to this country, the hostess explained to adults to put on their own oxygen masks before those of children. What use are we when overwhelmed, faint, oblivious that we are plunging into the ocean?

So I used the machine on myself. I started with my hands. Veins like cheese from back home and skin as dry as a cat's tongue. I placed both children in a playpen with toys, food, iPads. Lying naked on my front, I stretched my hands into the machine for two rounds of stasis. Running from machine to children was exhausting. I turned up the music to drown out their cries. A strict rota of the most important areas: hands, face, breasts, at two cycles per body part, filled the day before my husband returned – giving me just enough time to tend to nappy rash and face wipes.

In time, the children fended for themselves, became so self-sufficient I could burst with pride. My structured use of the machine went a step further than stopping me ageing – rejuvenation! Supple, strong, soft. My energy levels bubbled over. I ran up and down the stairs two at once until time started to condense. Whoosh, I was at the top of the stairs without recalling how I got there. Swish, I was holding a bowl of egg-whites whipped into soft peaks, unrecognisable from the gloop they started as.

The children stared wide-eyed in wonder at who Momma was becoming. I remembered how to laugh. My old language bubbled out, filling the house with soft, throaty sounds of the sea.

When my husband came home early that day with his sour-faced sister, I couldn't hear what he said. I watched his small, tight mouth move. Saw the grey wisps in his little moustache that proved the growing gap between our ages. He shook his head as I pulled my face out of the special box, cheeks still tingling from the rays.

'But look how young I am! Feel my skin.'

He took a step back from me. His sister grabbed one child under each arm while crying and yelling at me. So jealous.

I felt light and free as if watching them all through a television screen. Until he touched my machine. Then I screamed and scratched, my lungs refusing to fill. I strained for my machine, my everything. He pinned my perfect body to the ground with one arm as he dialled emergency services with a hairy thumb saying, 'It's just a cardboard box, what the hell is wrong with you?'

I stopped wrestling and wondered if I could mould my body into thin air now, swerve out from under him and fly through the window.

As I stared at the backs of my hands, they faded completely. My feet melted into the carpet. I closed tissue-thin eyelids and accepted the inevitable.

In Case of Emergency, Pull Cord

This place is all I've ever known and all I'll ever need.

The escalator carries me down to my favourite underground line. I feel the pull of gravity. At the bottom of the escalator, my shoulders lower as my breath slows. It's not rush hour, so there are no crowds – plenty of breathing space. It's good to be home. Below.

I run my fingertips along the cool walls of the tunnel. It curves and divides into twin platforms. They look the same but travel in opposite directions. My feet make a choice and take me to the right, eastbound.

No one notices a quiet boy like me – not so young that they worry about who's looking after me, not so old that they're checking for jittery legs that say I just might jump onto the tracks.

~

Ezra's grey guard's uniform fits him as snug as if he was sewn into it. It curves gently over his stomach. With a full, dark beard and brown skin, he's like the negatives of an old photo of someone dressed as Father Christmas. I can't place his accent, but it's from somewhere far away. He's clever, like someone off the telly who always knows just what to say.

It took some courage to speak to Ezra the first time. I'd watched him for a while and took comfort from his routines along the rail tracks. I stammered, surprised at the sound of my own voice.

'If it's okay, can I tag along for a bit? I'm Max.' I curled the toes of one foot into the floor through my trainers.

'Of course. It's up to you,' he said, looking up from his papers. His slow smile looked like it had something to say.

Now, Ezra lets me watch him doing his daily tasks Below. In his hand, he carries papers clipped onto a black file. He makes notes and ticks them off as he walks.

I shadow Ezra on the days that he works on my favourite lines. Just for an hour or so. I study his relaxed manner with all the other passengers as he directs them this way and that, how he writes notes without even looking down, his steady pace in the chaos of rush hour. Whatever happens around us, his shirt rises and falls in the same regular rhythm.

Ezra doesn't shout. But he has the type of voice you can't hide from: each word seeps through and echoes long after he's gone home. I sit on a near-empty platform late at night and still hear the words he said earlier that day.

'Are you sure that's the direction you want to travel today?'

His questions sound like Thought of the Day on the noticeboard at the bottom of the escalators.

Ezra never tells me what to do, but somehow it feels like he's trying to.

As we stride up and down the platform together, my words spill out. Ezra seems interested in everything that I've learnt from newspapers and books left scattered on the train or overheard conversations. He doesn't seem surprised that I've memorised the depths of each station in feet from highest to lowest.

‘I wonder what you get from being deep down, away from it all?’ He focuses on me as if I’m going to tell him the lottery numbers.

‘I like being closer to the centre of the planet,’ I say, looking down at my white trainers.

Ezra taps his page with the end of his pen and nods.

‘It feels safer for you then.’

I don’t really know what he means, so I shrug.

(Something’s missing. Someone’s gone.)

I don’t need anyone or anything that’s not right here.

Ezra never asks how come I’m still Below or why I don’t have a family. But he does ask tricky questions.

‘What really matters to you?’ he asks now, in his low, warm tone.

He stops walking and turns to me, head tipped to one side. I don’t know the answer, so stare up at the announcement board and watch the seconds pass until he disappears.

~

Down here is like the entire world in miniature. Languages roll off tongues and scratch throats and hum tunes. Huge suitcases with zig-zag wheels disobey their owners. Groups of little kids in high-vis jackets link arms, squealing. The air changes from hour to hour, thick with musk, spice, sweat.

Opposite me, each station is named in turn on the platform wall. They belong together, like siblings. I read one per heartbeat by pressing two fingers to my neck. The carotid pulse: that’s the one to check whether someone’s still alive.

I climb aboard the train and perch on a seat nearest the doors. Opposite me sits the guy I often see on this line. He’s in his early twenties with hair flopped over his eyes, a dark beard, a faded T-shirt. His whole body is tense as he digs the nails of one hand into the back of the other. I’ve never seen him in any state other than agitated. I drop my head down and imagine joining up the black spots of the floor like a dot-to-dot. We rattle and rock along.

I'm not homeless. I'm stretching across my home, exploring its vastness in familiar order. I'm connected to everyone and everywhere in this city. On my terms. Almost invisible.

~

Two men get on board at the fourth stop along. They carry cans of extra-strength cider. Sunburn stripes the back of their necks, which are layered with fat like baby's thighs. The bald guy swaggers about the carriage shouting to his mate.

'You wouldn't bloody know you're in our country, look at the lot of 'em.' He sweeps his arm across the air in front of him. A lady wearing salwar kameez in the colours of a peacock pulls her young daughter close and stares out of the window into darkness. A young woman with braids turns to the men as my mouth loses all its moisture.

'Why don't you take a seat,' she says. Her voice is ice-cream smooth.

The bald man flashes a grin to his mate, then paces towards the woman and looms over her. I can smell his boozy breath from several seats away. He beckons his mate over with one curled finger.

'This bitch thinks she can tell me what to do, Lee.'

Lee bends down to eye level with her.

The woman looks around at the rest of the passengers. Her forehead creases for just a moment. Nobody moves. We stare at our feet and check our watches.

Lee leans towards the woman and whispers into her ear. His fat fingers reach out to one of her braids.

My legs are made of stone. I've swallowed my voice box.

An electronic voice announces that we are approaching the next station.

Our train slows with a sigh.

The bald man finishes his drink and crushes the can under his boot.

'Let me tell you...' he starts, stabbing the air with one finger.

The adrenaline reaches my limbs: I jump up and rush through the open train doors. Without watching, I hear the train pull away, taking its travellers out of reach.

My vision blurs as my head swims. The shush of the train has gone, and it's too late to help now. I feel weak like I'm just made of bones with not enough muscle to hold them together.

Above me, the departure board flickers. One row of letters blinks and shifts into a new order.

Brecton – 2m – on time

Palsall – 6m – on time

Act – soon – still time

I swish between worlds. I don't choose to; it just happens: time and place flip-flop, like floating in silence on the Dead Sea.

Then chunks of time are missing. I'll jump from early morning commuters in suits and scowls to the late-night lull of stragglers and singers. Now it's quiet – evening at a guess. My body feels cool, and my lip aches where I've bitten it.

Something other than hunger is growling inside me. I tap each finger in turn to my thumb and press my back against the tiled wall to check that I'm solid. A small insect lands beside me.

Once, I showed Ezra the molestus mosquito, which lives only Below. We squatted over a crack in the wall and stared at its spindly legs and vibrating body.

'It looks like the mosquitoes that live on the Surface,' I said, 'but time apart in evolution means they're now a different breed Below. It's adapted to living here – the darkness, the lack of birds to feed on.'

Its antennae quivered. Maybe it smelt what we could offer it.

'What do they make you think of?' said Ezra.

The mosquito was so tiny yet fed on humans.

(Blood and suffering.)

'Not much,' I said. 'They're just pretty cool.'

The mosquito next to me freezes at my breath. Alone. So different to the lines of ants who work together to make a feast, cleaning up the place as they go.

'How come you keep doing the same thing here,' Ezra asked, 'rather than spend time in the world out there?'

I wanted to please him with the right answer.

'I will try,' I said. 'I'm just not sure I'm ready yet.'

'You could experiment!' Ezra said. 'See what happens?'

But I had no need to change so carried on as usual, moving the conversation to discuss how bees dance their messages to each other.

Now I wonder where the woman with the braids is, whether she escaped beery breath and threats to make it home safely. I want to find her, alter the past, make a difference. Maybe *now* is the time to change?

I abandon my usual route and head for a different line. I've traced its course with my finger on the map before, but it's not one I usually ride because of where it travels. This is a line that switches between Surface and Below. Stop, Go. Dangerous, Safe.

I need to push myself.

Let's say there's a man who's scared of spiders. He shouldn't be, of course – not in this country anyway, but maybe his uncle told him they creep up people's noses at night and lay eggs that hatch in their brains, then eat their way out. Perhaps he started off avoiding dark cupboards or the space under his bed, just in case. But over time, he got so fearful that he stopped going outdoors, couldn't place one foot on the carpet, spent his time in bed scanning the walls for dark specks of movement until his eyeballs ached. That would mean he couldn't ever learn that spiders are fascinating, beautiful creatures. They'd exist in his head as terrible monsters with no evidence to tell him anything else.

They say the only way to stop being scared is to face a fear. He should make a list of actions from low to high fear levels, then practise doing them while keeping his breath steady. Like this: he says the word spider until that's no longer scary. Saying any word often enough turns it to gobbledygook – where does the word start and where does it end? Spiderspiderspider becomes derspy,derspy,derspy.

(Suicide, Sue, Wee, Side, sue weesidesue, weesidesue, weesidesue.)

The sounds lose their scariness that way. Then he draws a spider with a smiley face again and again until it isn't fearsome, just cute. Next, he cuts out a picture of a hairy spider and holds it in his palm until his heart slows to a steady dee-dum, dee-dum. By the end of it all, he reaches the top of his fear list. Now it's just a list. He leans over a hairy-legged invader, his breaths as steady as a sleeping dog.

What do I fear?

The Surface.

Judgement.

(Remembering.)

I'll watch the outside world from behind the safety of a window, knowing it's a temporary view. Hopefully before it gets too much for me, I'll be back Below.

The train tilts upwards. The pressure in my ears changes as if we've launched into orbit. None of the other passengers around me reacts to the slight change in angle, while I grip the metal arm of my seat and try to unstick my tongue from the roof of my mouth. Through the clear doors that link to the next carriage, I glimpse the agitated man. He pushes his fringe out of his eyes, frowning. His forehead shines with sweat. Then he drops his head into his hands.

We ease up to the Surface. Not in the safety of the main station where I wash and find discarded food, but outdoors in the city. Hazy sunlight filters through fingers of cloud. I squint and shift my gaze from sky to street level. Sharp-edged, metallic buildings bounce beams of light between themselves like chatter. Walls of glass leave no privacy for those figures behind. A round tower sits next to its oblong siblings, and I wonder if all the furniture inside it is curved too. Everything here is silver, sleek black or see-through. History wiped out to make way for the space age.

We rumble over a steel bridge that divides the city. I turn to look out of the window on the opposite side of the train. Here, older parts of the city crush together: red bricks, sash windows, decorated doorways huge enough for giants. One row of buildings covers centuries of time, but not in the right order. The ground level is crammed with ugly storefronts selling e-cigs and cheap booze. Men sit outside wrapped in old coats with their dogs. Cardboard signs plead for help.

I close my eyes and see a different sign. A letter in familiar looped handwriting. It says 'I'm sorry, I don't know what else to do.' It's lying on a bed, three feet away from a sight that

I don't want to remember: a shadow hanging from the light-fitting in the shape of someone I loved.

My arms slacken. My entire body rocks in time with the carriage. I half open my eyes. A poster on the wall in front of me says 'In case of emergency, pull cord' in six languages. It fades, and all I see are dancing dots of light that move further and further apart as I fall into emptiness.

~

The whirring engine has reduced to a soft hum in the stationary train. I stretch back into my body as if waking from hibernation. Fake yellow light floods the carriage – I've returned Below.

A robotic voice booms out.

'All change!'

But I don't know where to go in this new part of the system. I feel a kind of homesickness.

I walk through a tunnel to get to a more familiar line – I've had enough of the Surface for one day. A busker wearing beads and sandals strums his guitar. I scuttle past with no coins to throw into his hat as he sings 'He Ain't Heavy, He's My Brother'.

My throat starts to close as if it doesn't want to let air in or let any sounds out.

I hear the echo of Ezra's phrases.

'Good enough, is good enough. We can only do what we can.'

My body crumples by the side of the busker, and even though I don't cry because there's never anything to cry about Below, my face is tucked into my knees which are warm from tears that won't stop.

I have a brother.

I *had* a brother.

~

When I lift my head, time's passed. The busker is gone. My shoulder feels warmed as if he's been embracing me. Maybe singing to me that *I* ain't heavy.

I pull myself back up and follow my nose to the familiar line that heads westwards back across the city but remains underground all the way.

The platform is busy. An elderly couple hold hands and seem content just to be with each other. A girl in striped tights nods her head along to music pumped directly into her ears from a small device on her belt. A young guy sits on his suitcase with a book that I'd flicked through on the train once, reading just the first and last page as if the rest didn't matter. Now I ache to know the story.

There's the agitated man up ahead of me. He's standing on the far side of the platform nearest the tunnel in ripped jeans and a band T-shirt. I swallow away a bitter taste in my mouth as he paces back and forth, muttering to himself. His fists are clenched while his lips move with barely a sound coming out. He shifts his weight between his feet, rocking along with his strange speech. As the platform clock counts down to our train's arrival, he nods, nods, nods, opens his fist into splayed, taut fingers and takes a gulp of air.

Time warps now. Although the agitated man is standing right there, looking towards the space that will soon be a train, there's something else. A see-through version of him leaves the real version behind and lurches past the yellow safety line, arms by his side with translucent palms facing outwards – he leans forward slightly with his knees bent. The anguish drains from his face like he's just knocked back the first whisky after abstinence. I know what he's about to do. I don't know it as a thought or a guess or mind-reading. I know it in the pit of my stomach, in the chill of goose pimples, in the pulsing beat of my ears.

Time jolts back into place. The roar of the approaching train blows down the tunnel. I weave through the crowd, past the couple, the girl, the suitcase, with my eyes focused on the man who's edged closer to the yellow line, ready to step forward. Ready to jump. The train rattles inside my head while I push onwards. I elbow my way past bags and shoulders, all the time focused on the man I desperately need to reach. I've got to get him away from the track and screeching metal. I'm in touching distance of him as the front of the train comes into view. He steps across the line, knees bent – in real time now. I feel my arms grow longer, long enough to wrap around him, and I'm suddenly so strong, strong enough to pull him back, stumbling. My words spill from nowhere, about how none of it was his fault, he tried his best, he's allowed to have his own life now, as I clutch onto his shoulder. He blinks at me, teary-eyed, in shock but safe.

He opens his mouth to speak, and I feel a force so strong from inside him that it sucks me forwards. My body compresses and shoots straight into his jaws, like diving into the pool's deep end.

Darkness. Dizziness. Pain.

People gather around, hands on me. On the new me. Arms lengthened, chest crushed, face furry.

'You okay there?' asks the old man, still holding his wife's hand as his crinkled face searches mine with worry. I could count the lines around his eyes and mouth to calculate the number of years they have loved each other.

I look down at my long torso, my jeans, my band T-shirt.

The train has pulled in, and I nod to the couple that I'm fine, they can get on. The crowd disperses and leaves me gasping on the platform.

Not a lost child but a lost young man.

No, not a lost man but a hiding man.

Not a suicidal man, but a man wanting to escape guilt and grief.

And I remember.

I step back and lean against a pillar. The station names above track the stops on my route to university that I haven't attended for weeks, as I've been riding the underground trains day and night, eating leftover food, changing into lost property clothes left in the station.

I don't want to die.

But somebody died. And I didn't stop it.

I look around, hoping to see Ezra, but the station guard nearby has the wrong face. I crave Ezra's calm presence as we walk up and down the platform.

No, as we walked up and down the corridor. The corridor of the clinic. Because I was too scared to enter the therapy room and have him judge me. I didn't want to lose those few hours chatting about the world, my zoology course, books – anything that wasn't about my twin.

My brother left me a phone message, but I hadn't listened to it in time. I hadn't called him at home that day. Too busy getting on with my life since the last time he tried to end it all.

I was the big brother by six minutes – non-identical – but I couldn't save him no matter what I did. Midnight phone calls, visits to the doctors, bank transfers of my student loan. He just couldn't escape the darkness that told him this tunnel will never end, there is no light.

~

I head back through an archway to the escalator. My reflection returns my gaze in the glass sheen of the posters. On the way up, I press my hand against the warm handrail and notice how it moves along in perfect time with me.

Stop, Stop, Stop, Go

Three stops before the bus arrives near my home, and I'm sitting on my hands to discipline my fingers into good behaviour. The lady sitting in front of me has her chestnut hair in a loose chignon. Each section curls around the next like strips of bacon nestling together in a pan. Little wisps escape and beckon me. My fingers ache to trace over the shapes and smooth the hair into place. I bend forwards to apply more pressure to my trapped hands. As I do, I smell the remnants of her day and the shadow of last night.

My husband is perplexed. He misunderstands my tenderness for others, as of course a man would. Whilst he stomped about this morning, I noticed how deeply the ridges in his forehead indented; canyons carved from three years of marriage. The muscles of his forearm flexed with every other word, which boomed, sending capital letters rocketing into the air. I nodded along as I watched NEVER and MUST and EMBARRASSING ping against the wall and change direction like the screen of a neglected DVD player.

One stop away from home. I distract myself from the lady's hair by pressing my feet to the floor of the bus. Vibrations hum up my legs. All the passengers sway to the bass of the engine as the bus bounces along the unloved road. We are connected in rhythm.

Perched on his mother's lap, an infant stares at his own wiggling fingers. He dribbles with delight in the moment that is only now. I roll out my tongue. He copies, and we both giggle. His mother yanks a cloth from her bag and dabs at his saliva, tutting to teach him of shame.

We approach the bus stop near my house. Habit tells me to stand. I cross my feet over one another and stay seated, staring at their capacity to choose. I narrow my eyes so that rows of shops and buildings blur into a cartoon of colour. My muscles exhale. Seventeen of us rock gently together as the rumble becomes a roar, the landscape changing from greys to green, green, green.

The Price of Teeth

The Tooth Fairy stirs in his treetop nest.

At number seven, Lola tilts her slender neck towards the mirror. She perfects poses with her glossed lips pressed together. Her tongue explores the new space, running over the soft balloon that used to house her front tooth. Wobbling in Mum's red heels, she strides the length of her bedroom. Under her pillow, the minty evidence awaits payment.

The Tooth Fairy's furry limbs uncurl at the beckoning new scent – fresh blood. With click-clack claws, he shuffles along the branch. His twitching nose drinks in the fragrances from each bedroom window in the row of terraced houses below. His hind leg strokes against his pouch which holds a single stolen coin. Gluey secretions fill his mouth. His tongue darts over gums that will soon host his first tooth: the mark of maturity. He nestles in silence and waits for the room to darken.

Lola awakes to the snuffles of the Tooth Fairy as he pulls at her pillow. She props herself up on an elbow and watches him at work.

'You don't have any fairy wings,' she says, narrowing her eyes in the darkness to take in the strangeness of his form.

'I'm a good climber,' he replies, moving his long nose nearer to hers. Saliva drips from his jaw onto her pink bedspread. As he flicks his tongue up, a coin glistens in the light of the streetlamp. 'You're not supposed to see me. I'm not allowed to take the tooth now. I've failed.' He rests on his hind legs and lets the coin drop in front of him.

'You can have my tooth, I don't need it, I'm not a little girl,' says the little girl. 'Also, it's not kind to call anyone a failure, I bet you were doing your best. You can't get it right all the time, you know.' She frowns as she hands over the tooth from underneath her pillow.

The Tooth Fairy's tail starts to wag. He takes the tooth in his paws and stashes it into his fur for later. His saliva thickens once more.

'Once I have this tooth glued in, I will be a fully-grown fairy. I can give you a wish that will be granted first thing tomorrow morning. But you must never tell a soul.'

Lola's nightdress flutters in the breeze as her fingers wiggle along with her thoughts.

'Thank you. I wish for my mummy to be well again.'

The Tooth Fairy crawls along the edge of the bed, then hops onto the windowsill. His head tilts sideways.

'Whatever that takes?' he says. His antennae vibrate.

Lola beams and clasps her small hands together.

'Yes, that will be perfect. Good night.'

The Tooth Fairy hesitates, then climbs out of the window into the dark as Lola's hair starts to shed onto her pillow.

The Accidental CEO

At Infinity Insurance, receptionist Maisie waited to welcome the new lead risk assessor, head-hunted by an agency. The man who approached wore a long woollen coat with a raggedy collar pulled upwards, shoes that looked like they'd walked further than The Proclaimers, a panting dog by his side that could have been part wolf. This man had a presence, a solidity. Maisie straightened her spine.

'I've been waiting for you, sir,' she said. 'We've heard such great things about you. You know, about assessing risk?'

The man nodded slowly.

'Aye, there's plenty of that,' he said. 'No need to let things get to a certain point. Keep watchful wait and smooth away trouble before it starts.'

'I'm so sorry, I don't have your name, just your job title,' Maisie said, lifting up piles of paper strewn across the desk.

The man looked towards his dog as if it might answer for him.

'They call me *wise man*, on the streets at least. I left the other names behind. And this is Grit.'

'Mr Wiseman, of course.' Maisie's fingers fluttered at the ends of her hair. 'I'll let Mr Fulsome know you have arrived. Can I get you and Grit anything?'

Wiseman placed one hand on the top of his dog's head. His deep voice vibrated Maisie's paperwork.

'I had a feeling you were the kind of lady who would see just what was needed.'

Maisie flushed as she gathered coins from her purse to buy coffee and dog food. Wiseman followed her to a large conference room with windows that looked out onto more rooms.

'Cages of glass,' said Wiseman, as he eased himself into a leather chair at the head of the table. Grit settled his head down onto his front paws until the door swung open. Fulsome beamed, then crossed the room in a zigzag line as if the floor were hot coals.

'Aha! Here he is then,' said Fulsome, placing his sweating boy-sized palm into the large, dry hands of the man he presumed was his new lead risk assessor. 'Wiseman, I've got four minutes. Let's blast some ideas before Board today. We're the sixteenth leading insurance company in this region, as you can see on the poster here. *Better Insure than Unsure.* Tell me what you've got to get us to fifteenth, or sod it, to get us to the top ten.'

Wiseman leant back in his chair, staring at the poster. He touched his ring finger where there was no longer anything to spin.

'You can't predict or prevent the future, so people shut down as if nothing bad could happen to them,' said Wiseman, turning to face the younger man opposite him. 'But if we all had our eyes open to the darkness slipping under the door, under our skin, then we'd be frozen in fear.'

Fulsome tap-tapped into his phone, 'I see, so change their emotional state to enhance expenditure! They've got to believe it could happen to them, but not be a big girl's blouse about it.'

His phone pinged.

'Let's go to the shop floor. And love the beard, by the way, very on trend that hipster look, like you just don't give a shit!'

Gurgles escaped from Wiseman's stomach as they walked down the neon-lit corridor.

'Hungry. Just all the time, so hungry.'

'Love your style,' said Fulsome, jittery movements in his arms and legs doubling his energy consumption, 'Yes, let's go get 'em – hungry for success, every day ending in 'y'!'

From the viewing platform, both men looked down onto the basement call-centre filled with more than a hundred workers in small booths, each wearing a headpiece. Wiseman dropped his coat to the floor as he descended the steps, then paced up and down the aisles. The workers continued with their scripts, despite the tall man in crumpled clothing and strange smelling dog cocking their heads to one side next to them: to stop would incur docked wages.

By the time Maisie arrived with coffee, croissants and dog food, Wiseman had filled a third of his notebook with left-leaning letters. Back on the viewing platform, the scripts of the call centre workers melded into one chant.

'You are treating these people like battery hens,' said Wiseman, sprinkling his knees with flakes of pastry as he talked and ate at the same time. 'They say you can taste the difference with free-range, that the stress hormones in the battery chickens changes their very substance.'

Fulsome drank his coffee in one gulp like a shot of whisky. 'You mean we should set them free? Walking and talking? To increase productivity? Free range.' He scanned left to right with a furrowed brow.

'And you have them in a suit and tie,' said Wiseman, feeding the rest of his brunch to Grit. 'On the telephone? Those ties are like ligatures.' He undid the top buttons of his shirt, pulled at the frayed edge of a T-shirt underneath.

'Good catch, Wiseman, don't want to get sued if one of them ends it all in the staff toilets.'

Wiseman blinked three times in a row, inhaled as if to speak, then clamped his teeth together and rubbed the fur above Grit's tail which wagged slowly.

It was unthinkable that Infinity Insurance would allow 111 staff members to be off the phone at the same time, but it happened while Fulsome was grinning at his notes at all the changes that would shoot his company into the stratosphere of top insurers.

The speech that Wiseman went on to make from the viewing platform would increase company profits by 263% in the following quarter. It contained phrases such as 'speak to your callers as if they were that one kid at school who showed kindness to you'. Jaws slackened at Wiseman's plea to 'ditch that script for the first ten minutes. Find out about the person's loves and life, their hardships, their dreams. Above all, connect and show compassion.' He ended the speech, his voice cracking, 'Help people to feel safe. That's all any of us want.'

Mid-afternoon in the boardroom, rain slashed against triple-glazed windows as twelve senior managers and the chief executive stared at Wiseman.

Mr Archibald Hardy, CEO, cleared his throat before each sentence and had the shakiness of a body that had worked long past retirement age.

'And where exactly did you build your portfolio of work, Mr Wiseman?'

Wiseman looked at each staff member in turn.

'I must tell you all, I've learned more on the streets than in any so-called job.' He leant forwards on the table, and half the board members moved ever so slightly forward too.

'You are living off people's fear, but they are used to living with it – it hounds their dreams and leaves them shaking and drinking and clutching their stomachs every day. They need to feel that they have belongings, jobs, lives *worth* protecting.'

Fulsome picked at the edges of his cardboard coffee cup. 'We've got to big them up to catch them.'

A small blonde woman stretched up to the whiteboard at the end of the room and wrote *Big Them Up* and *Word on the Street*.

The ancient CEO joined his palms together as if in prayer.

'This man has obviously been putting the hours in, getting down in the nitty-gritty, dressing as they do to *think* as they do. Excellent. We can't make money from depressives, quite right.' Despite his enthusiasm, no colour showed in his cheeks as his weakened heart struggled to pump blood around his system – sixty-six days after this meeting, it would stop completely.

'What are your suggestions for efficiency?' asked a middle-aged man still leaning back in his chair with his hands behind his head. 'I don't see long chats to customers and staff mingling around talking about their tattoos and large televisions as a way to cut costs.'

Wiseman poured a glass of water and drank slowly. The questioner's arms eventually dropped down into his lap as he waited for a response.

'Only have people here who choose to be here. If they want to walk out of the door, with no reason, and no warning, then let them go. There should always be the choice to escape.'

Everyone turned to Mr Hardy, who now had his eyes closed in concentration.

'Yes. A new clause for the contracts. Call it the Freedom Clause.' He opened his eyes and grinned. 'We won't have to pay any redundancies, no long-term sick leave, no parental leave. My goodness, man, you're spot on! Let's give them their freedom.'

The tension broke as everyone chuckled and repeated what had been said. The lady with the marker pen wrote *Freedom* on the board, tried to draw a dove, then quickly rubbed it out with her finger.

'Speaking of which, it's three o'clock,' said Wiseman. Time for Grit's walk.'

He left the room, quickly followed by Fulsome.

'I've got the keys for your office – twelfth floor! You've made it big. Ensuite, great view.'

'The kind of office you could live in,' said Wiseman.

'I just knew you'd be a workaholic. Yeah, you can crash out there and work all night. Exec board tonight, seven o'clock.'

That evening, Wiseman was taken up to the top floor of the building for an Executive Board meeting at the request of the ailing CEO. There had been frantic emailing, texting and micro-meetings in the previous three hours about the genius ideas of this new staff member, who went to De Niro levels of method acting to understand the market.

The penthouse suite was decorated like a Victorian parlour. Old men shouted into one another's ears while smoking cigars under deactivated alarms.

Fulsome moved his bird weight between each leg.

'I'll have to leave you here – I'm not allowed to stay. Great job today. Inspiring stuff. I'm off to blog about it.'

Wiseman caught his arm.

'There are no women here. No people of colour. The higher we come, the lower we go.'

'I hear you,' said Fulsome, winking. 'No problem. Girls, bit of ethnic, and getting high. I'll sort you out for tonight. Legend.'

~

Thirteen weeks later, Grit sat behind his owner on the rooftop terrace, wary of the sixteen-storey drop below, yet still wagging his tail. Wiseman was named CEO of Infinity Insurance at his boss's demise. In his office lay neat rows of items he accrued but had no further use for. He had written a note to Maisie and one for Fulsome. Profits continued to rise, workforce ticked more smiley faces on their feedback forms, twenty-two per cent had walked out of the door to do something they had always dreamt of.

Wiseman held his leather bag filled with stacks of fifty-pound notes. Nobody was surprised when he informed them he did not have a bank account, that he would be paid in cash.

'You have to know when to say enough is enough,' he said to Grit.

Wiseman looked directly down at the city below. Then he shook his bag over the edge of the building and watched as the notes floated down onto streets that would soon be home again. They blew this way and that in the breeze, with an equal chance of landing anywhere.

Birthday Present

He'd said it was Botox in those injections.

It wasn't.

I forced out giggles with a gin and elderflower scent. Hazel and Kate sat on the cream sofa opposite, straight-backed and skinny like we were still at school. Their locked jaws watched me finish off my birthday chocolates and suck each finger in turn. They gifted me a raspberry pashmina large enough to cover any flesh my dress forgot. Geoff twitched in and out of the living room. His fingers ran through his hair like he was stroking himself for being such a good boy. The heavy scent of his aftershave mixed with bourbon. Then in came a nurse, all cheekbones and vanilla.

Already numbed from lunch-time cocktails, I hardly felt the needle slide under the pouch of my cheek. I pulled the pashmina tight around me as icy liquid spread like fingers across my face. My eyes closed. Kate's voice chirruped away an octave higher than mine somewhere several miles away. My tongue throbbed, then stilled; a lump of meat in my mouth.

Hazel poured more Prosecco, and we tinkled our glasses together in clumsy pairs.

‘To health and happiness,’ said Geoff as he rubbed his palms down the legs of his tailored trousers. His eyes barely left my face, despite Hazel’s low-cut top.

Three bottles later, I was lying in bed exploring my face with my fingertips. I poked a finger into my mouth and touched a stranger’s tongue. I dreamt about having my wisdom teeth removed.

The next morning, I tuned out from my hangover and started to prepare pancakes. Six was my lucky number. Geoff was at work. He had already sent his morning text to check I was out of bed. I swirled a heart of syrup on each pancake, then zigzagged them out with gloopy lines. Heaving onto the armchair, I craned a large spoonful into my mouth. A foamy touch to my tongue was quickly followed by a warm creeping drip. I spat it out without meaning to. What kind of out-of-date crap was that? I gulped a mouthful of orange juice. Thick water with floating particles slurped around. I spat it back into the glass.

I could no longer taste.

With my pulse beating in my ears, I googled the symptoms. Taste disorders could create a variety of tastes: salty, rancid, or metallic. I had no taste at all. Infection, radiotherapy, surgery, head injury. None of the above. I touched the site of injection on my cheek as I looked at the only photograph of Geoff and me on display in the house. It showed only our faces, with me half hidden behind my veil.

I lost five stone that year. Geoff started to get holiday brochures out and fold corners over. He hummed and smiled to the apps on his phone. Hazel and Kate cooed while they poked at me and lifted my blouse. I waited until I was alone, then cried as I drank thick invasive mush for breakfast and lunch. My tongue weighed heavy and foreign in my mouth.

The hours passed through a strict timetable of cleaning. Busy, busy, busy. Nothing smelt right. Nothing really smelt of anything. There was a faint angry scent from bleach that I craved. The bathroom sparkled. Each surface glowed. My cracked hands burned.

I lost more. I lost count. My skin greyed, and my teeth yellowed. Geoff stopped pestering me to go out. Folds of empty skin hung like old clothes. Dreading infection, I washed and washed but never felt clean.

The hospital ward was at least polished every day. Not by me. I couldn't move much now. The drip was my lifeline. Sweet relief to bypass my mouth. As the doctors talked and nurses fussed, I watched cartoon Marilyn Monroes dance in my peripheral vision. She wore only Chanel N°5 to bed. I wished I could smell it or taste her lips of strawberry lace and marshmallows.

~

They say that birthdays with a zero in them are different. They push us to get round to things. Things like divorce, rented apartments, lists of what matters and facing our fears. I light four candles on the supermarket chocolate cake, one for each decade. The heat from the flames causes a little of the topping to melt down the side. Without thinking, my finger rescues the brown drip and hovers in front of my face. My tongue will tell me this is gloop, stodge, sticky, gummy, gross.

'This is chocolate. It is rich and warm. Its sweet cocoa caress feels like the hug of a missed auntie. It melts into your mouth like it wants to be eaten. It smells like a kiss from a man who bothers to say I love you.'

I listen to my memories and cut myself a large piece.

Davey, Plastic Jesus and the Holy Spirit

'Bad things happen to bad people,' says Pappa as we kneel to pray. He doesn't say what happens to good people like Mamma. Nobody says what happened to her. But I already know.

I press my hands together as tight as I can and sneak a peek at my sister. Jessica thinks God loves her, but he gave her curly hair that gets knotted, and she can't even see the Holy Spirit like I can.

'What about baby Jesus? It was pretty bad for him in the end, even though he was good.' I hold my arms out to my sides like I'm nailed to wood and roll my eyes back, but only cos I know Pappa's eyes are shut. His voice sounds funny these last few weeks, as if he's been gargling with glass.

'Jesus died for our sins, Davey. Remember the special name for the day he died? *Good* Friday. Praise the Lord. He's here in the hour of our need.'

I nod. Jesus looks down from the huge plastic cross on the wall. He winks at me; I wink right back. I guess his superpowers meant the nails didn't hurt. Oh boy, I know how he might have done it! Maybe he had magnetic hands, and that's how the nails stayed in while he tricked the baddies that he was dying. Jesus was good at playing pretend.

I side-eye Pappa. He strokes his moustache over and over like he's trying to make it feel better. Before we came to live by the church, he wore his plastic suit and special helmet like the rest of us, so he didn't look like Pappa at all. But we're safe here: we let our arms and faces go naked. In this hall at the back of the church, the dust is probably hair and skin of holy people, plus little bits of the Body of Christ, which is the proper name for the wafers at Mass. We're breathing in the good stuff. It's not being a cannibal or zombie if you're Catholic. I checked. It was worth being whacked, just to be sure.

Pappa ends prayer time with, 'In the name of the Father, the Son and the Holy Spirit.' There's so much I could tell him, but you have to learn the Grown-Ups code if you don't want the sting of a belt on the backs of your legs. When they say, 'Always tell the truth, boy,' what they mean is, 'Give me the Right Answer,' which oftentimes isn't the truth at all. Let's say you start seeing the Holy Spirit. I don't mean imagining it with your eyes screwed up like when you try to picture your guts wriggling under the skin of your belly after you eat. I mean properly see it. The best thing to do is K.I.T.Y – keep it to yourself. I made that up. Plastic Jesus's mouth curled into a smile when I told him that one. The thing is, the Holy Spirit is here just like Pappa said it would be. But he can't see it wrapping around his neck, making his eyes bulge. It's bright yellow. Not daffodil-yellow or crayon-yellow but stare-into-the-sun-till-it-hurts yellow. It doesn't say in the bible, but the Holy Spirit sure has a taste! It tastes like when you run your tongue over the bumps of a battery.

Pappa heads off to a meeting with the others who moved here to be with God. I'm stuck with my sister. I whisper *K.I.T.Y.*

'That isn't even a real word,' says Jessica.

'Oh, it's a word just for me. You wouldn't get it.'

She's drawing pictures of Jesus, and I don't bother telling her that she's made him look too serious – he's actually a good laugh. The Holy Spirit sneaks up around her and settles in a cloud over her head, changing her hair to a neon-bright shade like the stripes on my old trainers. I rush over to the blinds and shut them to see if Jessica glows in the dark, but she ruins it by switching the lamp on next to her. That would be a cool superpower. You could go out in the middle of the night and play hide and seek, looking for the glow. Or read comics under the covers. I blink a couple of times then the Holy Spirit has disappeared. It'll be back. I'm good at knowing about stuff before it happens. That's why I know where Mamma is. But K.I.T.Y.

When a bad thing happens, sometimes you can try to undo it. Like the first time the Bad Stuff leaked out, and nobody on the news told us. They tried to clean it up like nothing ever happened. But people started getting sick. Well, Mamma had spilt red wine on the carpet. It must have been the communion wine, the Blood of Christ. I don't know why she had it; maybe she was keeping it safe for the priest. Anyway, Mamma was on her knees trying to get the stain off the carpet because this place isn't ours, and we could get in trouble. We left our old house behind – it wasn't going to be okay for much longer there, not with the Bad Stuff in the air. Mamma scrubbed and scrubbed, but that stain was still there, the size of my hand. Pappa was at a meeting. He wasn't going to be happy when he saw that red mark. Mamma rolled back and sat on the heels of her feet like she used to when we played board games back home.

'There, that's better,' she said, staring right at the red stain like she couldn't see anything at all. I thought about how maybe it didn't come out because it was Jesus's blood, more special than most. She went out into the yard, just standing there with her arms crossed, staring at the sky. I watched the stain as it got bigger: a puddle, wider into a paddling pool, then more and more until the whole carpet was covered like lava. I jumped from the sofa to a chair to the back door using my floor-is-lava skills. I didn't know back then that I saw things no one else did.

'Mamma! Come and see – Jesus's blood is everywhere, like holy lava!'

She squinted at me then turned back to the lake, mumbling that I mustn't talk like that about Jesus, I shouldn't be bus-famous. I ran to her side and leant against her soft arm. I remembered those weeks before we packed up our things and squidged what we could into the car. It was mostly Grown-Up things. That was okay. I mean, I'm too old for superhero action figures, and I only ever read the last page in the books Mamma bought me. The old school buses were covered with posters that told us to Stay Safe and to Head to Havens. Everyone looked the same in their all-in-one suits and goggles – like angry bees buzzing about looking for flowers that don't grow anymore. I hated those buses. I hated leaving my mates, my bedroom, my turtle Benji.

The man on the side of the bus had white, white skin and white, white teeth and hair that looked like a wig. He had adverts on TV too. He said that God would look after his people, but he only meant some of the people with the right god, not like my best mate Amir. No way I wanted to be Bus-famous; nobody liked that man. Even Pappa swore about him once in front of us, said he was a self-serving prick who had no right calling himself a politician. I wrote that backwards for code on my comic so I wouldn't forget.

'Get to bed now, Davey-boy, before your father's back home,' she said. That's when I saw how weird Mamma's eyes had gone. I could see the lake in them. Not just a reflection of the water, I mean they *were* the water – blue waves instead of black dots. She turned away from me, back to the lake. 'The water's safe, you know,' she whispered. But it didn't seem safe; nothing did. I didn't understand what her water-eyes meant, but it felt like someone had reached down my throat and squeezed my stomach in their fist.

I never saw Mamma again.

'She's run away from Our Lord,' said Pappa. 'Straight into the hands of the devil and the downfall.'

I never told no one that Mamma didn't run away, that she's in the water.

We sit down for dinner around the little table in the kitchen. *Father, Son, and the Holy Sister*, I think. I must tell Jesus that one later, he'll have a chuckle.

The Holy Spirit is back and stronger than ever. It drips down Pappa, sliding down his skin so it almost looks like it's melting right off like Sunday roast beef from the bone. It's wrapped around Jessica's neck and flows up her nostril each time she breathes in until her nose glows.

'Focus on your food, boy,' snaps Pappa. The bread is not like it was back home – it's flat and dry, out of a plastic packet. W.W.J.D? What would Jesus do – I learnt that at Sunday School, back home. Well, Jesus would turn this rock-bread into soft floury loaves and tasty fishcakes! I stuff a forkful in my mouth and chew it as if it's the nicest thing I've ever tasted, giving my sister a big grin to show my mushed-up food.

'You're gross!' she says, pushing her own plate away.

Pappa slams his fist on the table.

'The Lord has provided, and you ungrateful children shame me with your behaviour! Eat your food with humility and the gratitude it deserves.'

I keep my eyes down. That's when it hits me.

The Holy Spirit never comes to me. I turn my left hand over under the table. Not a speck of yellow. Pappa and my sister have the Holy Spirit in their eyeballs. I need to check.

'May I be excused,' I ask. Pappa grunts his reply.

I run to the little mirror in the downstairs bathroom. There's no Holy Spirit in my hair, around my neck. I pull at the skin under each eye. No yellow swimming about, trying to cover up my black dots like the others have. Why does it not want me?

Bad things happen to bad people.

Whatever's happening in our old town, in all the towns, is it going to get me? Maybe God is cross that I haven't been holy enough. Maybe he doesn't like me having fun with Jesus?

I stick my face right up close to the mirror until my breath makes a little cloud. When I rub the smudge away, something has changed. My eyes. They aren't yellow. There are little blue waves inside. Like Mamma's.

I might be a kid, but I know what happened. I don't want to know, but I know it anyhow. Pappa was mad about the blood-carpet, about the holy wine. He hurt her. The blood pool wasn't Jesus's; it was Mamma's. I saw it before it happened. Then he threw Mamma in the lake.

The water wasn't safe; it was too late for her. Is he going to throw me in, too?

Even though I hear Pappa shouting for me to come back in for prayers, I ignore him, too busy running out to the lake with Jesus on the plastic cross under my arm.

Mamma wasn't telling me the water was safe for her. She was telling me it was safe for me.

Something's coming, and I reckon it's not the Holy Spirit after all.

I push out into the water, my clothes feeling heavier with each step as if they want to pull me down. I can hear Pappa's rough shouting; I can't tell what he's saying no more. I'm up to my waist, my armpits. But the heaviness pulls me down. A glug of water gets into my mouth, and I sick it back up. *The water is safe, the water is safe.*

My legs hurt and I realise I've never tried to swim with clothes on, it's too hard. I'm so tired. I want to sleep, to stop, to sink under and find Mamma at the bottom of the lake. The water sucks at me, sings to me. The cross bobs on a wave. I turn it over and look straight at Jesus. His arms are out wide as usual as if he's saying, *Let me carry you.* I fling myself on top of the cross and wriggle out of my trousers. He holds me. I float. I scrunch my eyes tight and don't open them even when there's a flash of light so bright my eyelids feel burnt, the taste of metal stronger than ever, one million batteries stuffed into my mouth. I hold onto Jesus and know that in three days' time, they'll find me, as if I've come back from the dead.

Leftovers

My mother-who-never-mothered-me has died, and I don't know what feelings to have, so decide not to have any. Lily sits on my knee in the council flat as we rummage in tatty boxes that hold things she kept, long after getting rid of me.

We divide items into two bags – one for the charity shop and one for the bin.

Patches of mould stretch from the ceiling down the walls as if trying to reach my mother, who died alone in her chair. Only the damp walls cry.

I search for something that would poke a memory. But these are leftovers of a stranger. No secret picture of me as a toddler. No unsent letter saying she was sorry. I tell Lily, 'You can take one thing to keep.'

In the rubble of magazines and pens and empty fag packets is a statue of a spaniel made from coal. We never had a pet. I pass it to Lily, who clutches it in her hand in silence.

The window looks out onto the bricked back of a shop. Yellowed nets hum of nicotine. The museum of my mother slowly fills the bag due for the bin – charities deserve better. I wonder if she shrank over the decades. I picture her feet dangling from her chair, unable to reach solid ground below.

A sensation is moving up from my guts. It is old; it takes its time. I grab some tissues from my coat pocket. Anger rises up through my body and into my mouth. I spit it onto the tissue. Dark, sticky puddles wriggle about as if surprised to be out in the open. We watch tentacles try to leave the tissue and make their way back into me. Lily grabs an old newspaper, and we wrap the anger tightly with layer after layer and secure it with an elastic band. It struggles for a short while, then sags in my hand. I throw it in the bin bag with the rest of the things I wish to leave behind.

I feel like I've lost a stone of weight. And want to cry.

My mother has died.

The Never-Quites, Never Quite, Never

The first of the Never-Quites to appear to her is back again. The young guy from the video shop with his River Phoenix fringe grins while he leans against her sofa. Esther sweeps past him to refill her Aldi Prosecco. The scent of Lynx Africa follows her. The soft down on her arms stands on end.

Esther makes her husband green tea. He's on a detox or a vegan now or worried about the virility of a virus. She craves a cigarette. Like the one she'd shared with video-shop boy, one Doc-Martened foot against the shop's wall. When she'd passed it back half-smoked, the cigarette had touched his lips and made her jealous.

The Never-Quites don't age. Don't disappoint. Don't want to impregnate. They can't touch her, but oh, that's so much better – that *almost*.

Esther unlocks the back door while her husband's tea steeps milk-free and unsatisfying. Out by the willow tree sits one of her favourite Never-Quites: the girl with too much eye-liner who'd worked for the Student Union and frowned about Issues with a capital 'I'. Three snakebites and black later, there'd been something. Or nothing. But maybe something that started and ended with a hand on her face and *you're pretty* or *you're prissy*, and Esther had been so unsure which that she'd run back to her three metre by two metre student cell and made herself sick into a wastepaper bin.

After Netflix and Facebook and goodnight, Esther tiptoes downstairs and nestles on the sofa. She'll tell her husband it's the rattle of his snores, but the rattle is in her bones. In her cells.

Another Never-Quite will show up if she's patient. From the bus. Or the library. Or that work party where they'd all worn wigs, and for a couple of hours, she'd felt like someone who wasn't shit.

She waits: the good kind. The kind that tingles, that teases, that pulls your guts upwards in longing.

The Never-Quites cause no fuss but being observed is enough. They nod from the corner of the room as she folds school uniform that she hasn't bothered to iron, using her warm hands to soothe away creases, or as she rubs cream into hands that have roughened and toughened into her mother's. But they never forget the girl she was and all she could have been.

Semaphore

That first summer on the island, my sister and I became amphibious. The boggy marsh squelched under our toes on the way to the lake. In vests and pants, we waded out fearlessly. No longer boy and girl. Submerged in liquid as pure as the holy host, we held our breath and waited for the other to surrender. We burst out of the water as twins in tandem – no need for a winner. Here, my words flowed as easily as the water around my shoulders.

Back in the house, the heaviness returned. Our parents' history shouted from the walls. Sound refused to leave the safety of my closed mouth. At dinner, we sent messages through movements of our fingers: *he's angry* or *let's go to the water*. They never noticed.

Mother dug the earth in clothes she no longer cared for. We watched her frown and sweat, fighting the land instead of our father. Lines of stone failed to hold back the water. All her hard work drowned within days. The sharp notes of father's whistle carried through the skies even when his heavy boots were out of sight.

We lost the code of our hands when my sister escaped to the mainland for boarding. My stutter sent me sprinting from school; she had potential. Her neat bags lined the hallway for the start of a new term. I pushed past her and ran until my breath burnt. As if I hadn't heard her cry.

I look at these large hands of mine as they inject escape into a vein. The rugged red hills of my knuckles from punching walls. I remember how small my sister's were. How they fit inside mine like a doll's.

Sometimes I sign, *let's go to the water*. But no one here speaks my language.

Six Decades of Savouring

The boiler's death rattle shook the walls just as snow started to sprinkle over the moorlands. Ernest laughed, rubbing his beard rhythmically as if he wasn't surrounded by silence. Shuffling around the cottage, he opened each window one by one. To live meant to feel; draught or love, it was all part of the package. Wheezing, he surrendered his torso to the armchair. His whisky-in-waiting was out of its long hibernation. He sniffed the fumes then poured a generous liver-full. It tasted as dark and heavy as his oak dresser. Lex kept a keen eye on the process, wagging his tail in Morse code. They held eye contact for a moment. Shivering brought on a strange alertness, as if he was waking up from a six-decade sleepwalk. He would be unmedicated – himself at last, whatever that brought. Images streamed behind his eyelids. He watched the show.

~

The whole family crammed around Nana's television to watch *Omnibus* on the night of the moon landing. Ernest nodded along to the commentary. His eyes flickered to Dad's serious face. He was close enough to lean on. Ernest had memorised facts about Apollo 11 and its crew. Pacing his nuggets of knowledge, he announced one piece of information every half hour.

Dad stared at the television. Mum fluttered about picking things up and putting them back down again. Just for tonight, he could stay up as late as he wanted.

'Great men do great things,' said Dad, rolling a cigarette with one hand.

He often talked about his wartime heroes, eyes wet as he recalled Grandad Charles and what he did for the country.

George, two years younger, pouted and kicked as he was sent to bed. He left behind the model rocket he was making from ice-lolly sticks.

'He's all hands and no brains, your brother,' said Nana, passing round the limp tongue sandwiches for the third time. Avoiding the offer, Ernest patted the sweet chalky cigarettes in his back pocket. On his way to the toilet, he crunched the rocket flat with his growing feet.

~

Placing his emptied glass down on the table for the fourth time, Ernest inspected his hands. Someone else's gnarled old fingers looked back at him. He pulled his sleeves down over them. Heartbeats galloped along with his thoughts. Through his shirt, he felt the rugged scars of surgery. As he tried to swallow, he could feel every tablet he had forced down over the last two years. They stacked up in his throat like stubborn smarties. His head moved slowly to the right to keep up with the spinning room. It was not unpleasant. Creaking his frame out of the chair, Ernest headed to the kitchen. Out of the top right cupboard, he pulled down his box for the week – a smorgasbord of tablets in timetabled rows. He let the coloured contents trickle into the bin as if out of an unwanted goody bag at the end of a party. Lex stuck to his side as he lumbered back to the armchair and felt the call of gravity on his eyelids.

~

The old drowned quarry three miles from this childhood home was the perfect place to dive. When the future had stretched out to the horizon, sticky summer days were filled with his friends in the water. As adulthood entered his muscles, Ernest saved his wages to fund third-hand diving equipment. The freedom of his summer water-world washed away violent memories of his father's fists. He became weightless. One July morning, his diving partner Jimmy had failed to turn his oxygen tank to the correct setting. Deep in the water, a pleasant fogginess turned to panic – he could not breathe. Signalling his need to surface, Ernest saw his fate in his friend's eyes. They rose up through the water together. The journey lasted seconds and days. A strange stillness filled his anoxic world. It didn't matter if he died. Hauled from the water, hot acidic waves erupted from his mouth onto the grassy bank. Worried hands and faces gathered around him. He brushed them away, then headed home, wiping his lips with his sleeve without looking back.

~

Ernest swirled whisky around the glass. Its smell warmed his nose as wind invaded the living room. He looked from wall to wall. Each was bare.

'Got no pictures, Lex. Nothing pretty.'

Books, papers and journals were tossed together. Squinting and leaning forwards, Ernest could not recognise what pieces of work lay around him. Years of isolating effort seemed like nothing more than dusty wiggles on a page. He watched as the lines danced around into new shapes and words. They no longer belonged to him. He smiled.

~

Once George's pottery designs had started to sell, all judgement was erased from the story. Mum and Dad covered every flat surface in teapots and dainty unused saucers. No need to turn them upside down to know their second son's signature was there. That was as much writing as George could manage. But that didn't matter anymore. George married a girl from the bakery and moved across town to a sturdy house by the park. They made three children named after soap-opera stars.

~

The shivering stopped. Ernest pulled at his collar as the air in his struggling lungs seemed to heat up. A gurgling cough stole his breath. His numbed hands released the whisky glass, which rolled on the debris below. Cock-eared, Lex briefly raised his head. As the coughing faded, he tucked himself back under Ernest's feet where he belonged.

~

There had been a woman, Margaret. She had teased him gently with her velvet skin. Ernest attended the same college lectures as her and spied on her shoulders from the row behind. As she spoke, he held his breath to hear those perfect vowels he could never reproduce. His eyes barely lifted from the ground, so his ears did all the work. She was clever. She did not fill her pockets with scraps of knowledge or practise her answers in front of a mocking mirror. Ernest never got to taste her mouth but guessed it was the bittersweet flavour of sugar on grapefruit.

~

In the darkness of early evening, memories slowed and merged. Ernest could feel his tired heartbeat throb in his ears. He no longer remembered in pictures but in smells and tastes and touch. The musky warmth of Mum's eau de cologne as he sneaked a sniff while his bath filled. Sharp, salty stings from a packet of crisps stolen from the larder while laughing to tears with George. And the cold, wet welcome of submerging his whole self into water and drinking clear liquid that tasted of nothing and everything all at once.

Everything Must Go

When we eventually meet, it turns out he's a security guard with the flop of a belly over his jeans, not some hunky cop who deserved a second chance. But we've already signed the deal, and he's buying my kidney. We worked out a pitch to sell to the papers – 'whirlwind internet romance kidney donation'. As if I'd look at him twice. He wants to break into TV; I'm thinking they say you gain twenty pounds, so I tell him the smart money's on the internet.

The downtown clinic smells of drains covered with a spray that wants to be lemon but hovers somewhere around mosquito repellent. I'm hoping the guy in a white coat is legit. He looks like some scrawny adolescent who can't quite muster enough testosterone for a beard. He whips out a syringe that looks like the one the vet used to tranquilise Lucky when there was no point him suffering more.

~

I'm groggy, crying. This is seriously not something I ever do, so I sniff it up and orientate myself. My concrete legs don't obey the call to swing off this bed. There's a thin tube going into the back of my hand. I look down at the green hospital gown and remember. And I wonder what I weigh now I'm minus one kidney.

~

From the couch, I watch the unknowing blonde girls on MTV writhe to tunes I've muted. I squeeze my remaining eye half shut and watch gyrating blobs. The floor is decorated with painkiller bottles and antiseptic wipes. The giant TV I bought with my first organ cheque fills a quarter of the room. I'm shrinking. He'd explained that spleens do jack-all; people have them out all the time. I didn't like the name anyway, that ungracious 'spl', like a curse. I bought a treadmill, a posh one with buttons I don't understand. He had contacts, he said. I wanted an iPad, a Nutribullet, a rowing machine. I offered parts of my gut next. There's miles of the stuff in all of us – shit-filled tubes weighing us down. I didn't ask who would want them. I got more subscribers with each removal of an organ: a fair deal. Some offered cash for particular parts. I've lost track after that. There's so much waste inside I can do without.

I haven't seen him for a while. We've stopped making videos. There's nothing left to sell.

The air is thin up a mountain; I read that somewhere. You have to gasp and get used to it. You vomit and feel weird while these goats just trip trap vertically, laughing at you. My breathing sounds kind of scary since they took my left lung. I can't get to the bathroom where the scales are. But I'm pretty sure I've made my target weight. I don't know if the laptop is still streaming. I turn towards it and smile to my fans.

Dalmatian Readings 1984–1989

Mum did her Dalmatian readings on Friday nights after lights out. Neighbours paid a quid a go to stare at Pongo and say what they saw. At first, it was a wine-warmed laugh with her mates. Like Barbara, who said her husband worked away, but no one had seen him since the mines shut, and Joanne, who was more gum than teeth and never had a boyfriend. They sat around the dining table that we never ate at since Dad left, sharing their smoker's cough and mint Matchmakers. I was curled on the settee fake-sleeping, straining to hear above the sound of Dallas in the background.

'That one near his bum looks like an angry robot,' said Barbara.

Mum stubbed her fag into the glass bowl with more sharp edges than I could count and breathed out for a long time.

'Barb. You're scared of technology. Of the future. Of being replaced. And when you're scared, you lash out. Instead of being scared of it, be the future, get out there.'

I didn't understand at the time that you can have more than one feeling at the same time. Barbara's grief-rage-excitement cocktail just looked like what Dad used to call 'hormonal'. But she took Mum's advice and enrolled on a local computing course and ended up with more money than Ron ever made.

She bought her own Nissan Maxima and got a perm. She never mentioned Ron again.

Word got out to the neighbours, and the canine Rorschach really took off. When I got in from school, Mum would be studying a pile of books from the library, picking out sentences and underlining them in pencil, then typing them up on an electronic typewriter. She'd peel potatoes, staring into the backyard at the orange space hopper I was too big to bounce on, saying things in her funny not-from-Stoke-on-Trent-today voice.

'You're envisioning what you want to be' or 'the phallus is a symbol of strength'.

The more she used words they didn't understand, the more they could make it fit just what they wanted. Aunty Jean stopped wearing bras and shaving her legs when she saw a black blob on Pongo's soft ear as a butterfly – 'Change and freedom,' Mum said, dropping pound coins into the zip section of her purse now there were no more pound notes to fold away.

Along the way, it changed from being about what the dalmatian spot was saying to predicting the future. I don't know why. Maybe that's what we all really needed Pongo to be, something more dependable than mines and pottery factories. Something for the future, not the past.

It was Mrs Hummings, the lollipop lady, who started it off. She needed an operation that the women all lowered their voices to talk about, shaking their heads with their mouths in a straight line. Pongo trotted right up to Mrs Hummings and laid his head on her lap. Probably smelt the chippy dinner.

'Oh, bloody hell, look at his ear! It's a thumbs-up clear as day! Look at the big thumb shape pointing right up, Liz, I'm going to be okay.'

Nobody said that the thumbs-up could look like a thumbs down depending whether you were sitting in front of Pongo or standing over him.

Mrs Hummings was okay in the end; she started speed-walking a few months after her operation and set up a business taking people's dogs for walks with her niece called 'Pet Shop Girls', which was kind of funny even though they didn't have a pet shop.

Every Friday night got booked up, so Mum started doing readings on Saturday afternoons. People were catching the bus up from all the six towns. She even had two old ladies over from Cheshire who took their shoes off in the hallway, oohing and aahing over the scratched Minton tiles like they were in a museum.

On Sundays, I'd take Pongo for a big run across the park, none of this dawdling with women who stopped to gossip or touch flowers every few steps. He went wild for the frisbee, hurtling himself like this might be the last time. We'd run until my lungs burnt in a good way, then wrestle on the grass and pant. I knew it was all pretend, good for Mum to have to focus on, to feel better about herself. She started laughing more, crying less, sleeping in her bedroom again instead of downstairs. Stopped jumping so much when the phone rang.

I lay on the grass listening to Pongo's fast breaths, rubbing the soft skin of his ears. His tail flapped happily. I wondered if Dad ever thought of Pongo. Whether he missed him. Whether he'd ever come back. On the end of Pongo's tail, I caught sight of a curve of black that could have been a smile, a wink, a yes. Or the thick black line of a marker pen that crosses out words that you're not allowed to read because they're too secret, not for you to know.

What to Do When You Can't Do Anything

The consultant is still talking, fingertips poised on his desk as if he is about to play a concerto. Unsettling minor-key melodies fill the room, yet I feel nothing while I weep. Palliative is a pretty word. It masks a horror that should not wrap its spindly legs around my three-year-old. A greying moustache hangs over his top lip. I watch the curve of his tongue as he says that word again. His dishevelled hair flaps on his head as he nods along, looking down at his notes.

'Here are some leaflets on hospice care, support for you afterwards and so forth. The nurses will explain.'

Then it comes. Fiery and raw, the strength blasts up from my stomach and down my arm. I grab the back of his head and slam his face into the desktop, crunching his glasses into podgy flesh. The force of my thrust pushes his head right through the oak. Cardboard files of nameless others fall through the gap and trap him under their weight.

I press pause. A welcome silence holds me upright as the wall clock stops its countdown. Peering through the window, I see a world that I can't allow to carry on, not yet. Traffic is frozen into patient queues, a bird dangles in the air mid-descent.

Hope pours down my veins and pools on the grey tiles underneath my feet like spilled petrol on the driveway. I step out of the puddle and into the hospital corridor. The statues around me clutch clipboards, stare at phones, hold hands. My feet march to Ella's ward. I hate every pastel princess and tumbling clown painted on these walls, smiling down at our children's suffering.

In the first bay, a bony teenage boy is captured in the moment just before he unhooks himself from the tube going into his arm. The nurse caught striding across the shiny floor seems familiar. Her hair is scraped into a tight bun to help keep a smile on her face. My girl is curled up on a beanbag in the reading corner. She frowns in concentration. Wisps of new doll-like hair glow on her temples. In the stillness, I crouch down and try to find a smell that belongs to her. With my cheek against hers, I dream of a time before this. Of early Sunday mornings with her wriggling beside me, telling me jokes that make no sense. Both of us giggling without knowing why.

I place my hand over hers. I wish we could stay in this embrace forever – but this is not a forever I wish for her. I kiss her head and whisper my love to her. The words turn to diamonds, glimmering at the corners of her eyes and cascading down her cheeks. Reaching into her, I steal a small ball of cells and place them in the locket around my neck.

Back in the car park, I remove the parking fine from the windscreen and throw it with the others on the seat behind me. In the next row, a woman in crumpled clothes holds her hand across her brow as if that will help her recall where she parked this morning, perhaps before she earned the title 'widow'. Moments have changed us forever. I unpause the scene. The woman turns her head from left to right, scanning each row helplessly.

My foot vibrates against the pedal as I race back to the village. At the health centre, I swing into a space marked 'Doctors only'. The receptionist shakes her head at me, her red talons tapping against the glass between us as I march past and throw open the door that leads to the doctor's office. I unfasten the locket and place the nest of cells into my left palm. He jumps as I burst into the room. His jaw tightens as he recognises me. This man who sent me and Ella away again and again. Who told me to stop worrying. Maybe have a spa day. He mumbles some formalities while looking at what must be an interesting spot on the wall. I fake a stumble, and as he recoils from the discomfort of human contact, my left hand sneaks through his blue shirt and taut skin. Tucked under his stomach, his pancreas squishes against my fingertips as I embed the cells into their new home. I pull back and apologise with a smile. He will feel unwell for a while. His wife will call it work stress. By the time he turns yellow, it will be too late to halt.

On my way out of the building, I smash my elbow against the fire alarm. As the bells scream at the staff to get out, I slam my hand onto the fire door and seal it shut with the heat of my rage. They will know the panic and confusion of realising there is no way out. For an hour or two, anyway.

Back at the house, I drop my bags in the hallway and check for lights. My husband is still in his bed after a night shift. I hadn't told him about today's appointment. Over the last eight months, we have settled into a silence, swerving between stalagmites of unspoken words as we pass through the house doing those things that seem to need doing. He moved to the spare room.

I stride the stairs and plan the words I must say. They have done all they can do. This man who can sleep as though there is no crying to be done. Who plays golf as I pull out clumps of my hair that are no use to anyone. He stirs as I enter. We look straight at each other. I curl up next to him on the bed. He cannot read my face, and I cannot speak. His hand reaches up and touches my forehead, cups my chin. My face melts into his palm, and he reads the Braille of my tears. He rocks with sobs and holds me so tight I wonder what it would be like if I never inhaled again.

Anatomy of a Marriage

The scan confirms what I already suspect: my organs are in the wrong place. The doctor shakes his head at the computer screen.

'This explains the abdominal pain,' he says, turning the screen to us.

My brain is nestled beneath my belly button. Out of habit, I place my hands over it. When I press my fingers into dimpled skin, memories are provoked: a first kiss with barely-there softness, the salty tang of tears, the scent of her neck in the night.

My wife pushes her glasses up the bridge of her nose and frowns in concentration.

'How peculiar,' she says.

She stares at the screen, not me.

The doctor shines a torch down my throat. He finds my liver tucked into my palate. It must cause the bile that spills from my mouth after days of silence: *leave me then, I'm no good anyway.* A sharp stick to check if the bug of our marriage is dead or just faking.

Then clunks and whirrs of a CT scan. In the viewing room, students gather round, phones held high with red lights flashing. Through a headpiece, I hear their excitement, like chimps ambushing a monkey for meat. Instead of two hemispheres of a brain, they find my lower intestines coiled like a snake. No wonder my memory has been poor. It skews to the dark side, leaves me wallowing in faeces of self-hatred.

Once I exit the machine, I vomit a little, then walk out of the room, corridor, hospital, county – still wearing only my medical gown. I crouch in some grassland for camouflage.

Now I'm someone of interest. A superstar. A specimen.

I roll myself small and tight, bring the parts of me back together. None of the tests showed the location of my most important organ. Maybe I never had one. In crash-landing position, I clutch the back of my neck. My fingertips find a beat just above my shoulder blade.

Instructions for the Use of Sulphuric Acid for Aesthetic Purposes

Suitable for the following:

- You have one of those faces – not pale enough to be china-doll memorable, but not dark enough to cause clicking tongues in your unwelcoming town.
- Your features are placed just where they should be, like a child's drawing of a face.
- Your hair offers nothing more than a frame around your regularity.
- Colleagues' lips mumble and trip as they try to recall your name.
- This disinterest is more painful than the smash of a fist.

Equipment needed:

- A large glass bowl which echoes light from each brutal angle.
- Analgesics.

Instructions for use:

- Trickle the liquid into the bowl, allowing it to sing. *(Please note, the smell is both horrific and intoxicating).*
- Tie your tired hair at the nape of your neck.
- If the answer to the following question is yes, then lower the face you were born with into the bowl.

Is this product right for me?

- Would it be better to be seen for your ugliness than be ignored for your ordinariness?

See-Through

Jake slowly moves the shotgun across the nursery classroom, and my wrists are sore from the belt that ties them together. The little kids don't really understand. But they're scared because the teachers are clearly freaking out while pretending not to. Mrs Wainwright pushes crying children behind the toy kitchen, chubby arms out wide as if she can spread that fat further and protect them. I remember her leaning over me when I was half this size while I flicked through a picture book, longing for words, to not be a baby anymore. She had the kind of body you could use as a pillow. If you could tolerate touch.

I can't tell from the chorus of snotty sobs coming from behind the toy house where my little brother Archie is hiding. Miss Hubbins, who's shaking all over, looks over to me, mouthing my name 'Christie, Christie' like I might make this all disappear. She has her group of kids scrunched into little balls as if there's a hurricane coming. But he's already here.

Jake Roberts. Almost as tall as them at eleven. Dressed in an old suit that used to be his grandad's. When he texted me a picture of it, I didn't know how to reply. It's not like I'm his girlfriend. Or his mum. I'd messaged back a picture of James Bond. The shoulder pads in his black jacket couldn't make up for what he lacked in width. But the shotgun, nicked from his grandparent's farm, has changed him. Like he somehow weighs more, is solid. The see-through boy they called him. But for the past four minutes, no grown-up has looked anywhere except straight at him.

Ten minutes earlier, I'd heard Jake drag last year's shoes up the corridor. Swish-clump, swish-clump. He always walks like he's in a battle with gravity. His paper-thin body too long for his age would maybe float off without those clunking boots to grip him where he didn't want to be. Jake joined our class halfway through the year back when we were nine. Rumours spread about why he had moved from inland to live with his grandparents here; his vowels were as strange as his eye contact. The truth was too mundane to talk about. In the end, he faded out as grey as his hand-me-downs. I slipped out of the classroom and felt the warmth of Jake's hands as he tied the belt around my wrists on our way down towards the nursery block.

We were ghost friends. I explained that I could message him and meet up at the marshes. But in school, we had to see through each other. He never asked questions. We chatted online under different names. As Girl999, I sent messages that described the parts of my life that no one at school knew. It was as if I was talking to my phone, not a person; a not-too-bright robot that was programmed to respond 'no way' or 'that sucks' or 'same'. But we were not the same. He didn't have the burden and gift of talent. Or the worried hands of a mother stroking his hair at night while staring at the walls, saying everything would be okay when it never was. He didn't have a little brother to light up his mum's blank eyes, sucking up her time and love like a measly pet.

Jake's breathing as fast as a dog through his open mouth, hands shaky with adrenalin. He twists his torso around to look at me. The gun swivels with him, pointing at my chest. I realise that I don't know whether it's loaded or not. His eyes don't seem to focus properly; they jump left to right like he's playing a computer game. My spit tastes bitter, and my school shirt sticks to my spine. That's when I notice Archie's striped sleeve clinging to Miss Hubbins' thigh. His little body is tucked behind her for protection, out of reach.

Jake needed to make a name for himself. And I needed to wake Mum up out of her divorce coma, to unglaze her eyes so she could see me. I knew Jake's grandad had some kind of farm gun. To leave no digital trail, we met by the marshes a mile from my house. A kind of nettle-and-needles spot for the locals to pass out in. He listened with his mouth dropped down like a kid watching cartoons when I whispered about the power of a man with a weapon. How people take notice, take you seriously. Just like those social workers and judges didn't when he said he wanted to stay with his mum and dad, that they were doing their best. I told him he was too young to go to Youth Offending Institute anyway. He wouldn't have to hurt anyone. Just be noticed. Be known.

The large doors into nursery class are now barricaded by a blue slide. Knocks turn to thuds against the reinforced glass of the door. Panicked voices outside start the clock. I nod my head forward towards the children, trying to alert Jake to move on to the next stage. The fire alarms screech out, and I stifle a laugh that doesn't belong here. There will be firefighters, police, hordes of worried parents on their way.

One school break, I offered to do litter duty and wrote Jake's name down too. With bin bags in our hands, we completed a tour of the school. I went off the usual route and walked him down the side of the fencing to show him the nursery building. He still jumped when a seagull swooped, as if it was after him, not the scraps of lunchtime.

'That's where Archie is. Mum only loves him. She wishes I didn't exist.'

Jake squinted at the building. I noticed his Adam's apple sticking out.

'He ruined everything. Dad couldn't cope with the noise disturbing his work. That's why he left us.'

It took Jake a while to think about things. I liked to do things fast. Pulling at his sleeve, I showed him where the litter needed picking up. He couldn't get his arms to co-ordinate with each other, and watching him try to catch the wrappers and paper floating in the breeze irritated me.

'Sod it, let's go back,' I said.

As we trotted back to the upper end of school, I felt a satisfaction like a belly full of lasagne.

We'd agreed he would tie my hands up, and I could say brave things. Police would burst in and pull us apart, never knowing that really we were together in a way no one would understand. The rule was that he must ignore anything I said.

The headmaster Mr Sparks is shouting through the doors, asking what the hell is going on. The nursery teachers look at each other, waiting to see who steps up. At first, I don't even realise it's my voice that is shouting back. It sounds different, fake.

'It's Christie, sir. There's no one hurt. But he's got a gun.' I can't say his name out loud.

Jake lets out a small noise. He starts shifting from one foot to another. I remember a bear at Blackpool Zoo that had lived in a box for so long it just rocked and rocked when it was given a whole load of space that it didn't know what to do with.

Now I've broken the seal of silence, Miss Hubbins starts gabbling, her cheeks wobbling as she calls out.

'It's Jake Millard, Jake! Get us out, he's mental, he's got a bloody shotgun.'

Then she remembers her role and crouches down to the children's level, using her teacher's voice, saying again and again, 'It's okay, we will be out soon.'

I don't know if I can hear sirens or if it's just the ringing in my ears.

'What do you want, Jake?' calls Mr Sparks, his voice higher pitched than usual. 'Let's have a chat. Put the gun down and come to the door, mate. Let's sort this nonsense out.'

Jake's shoulders stiffen at the word 'nonsense'.

Some of the children feel the relief of hearing our headmaster's voice. They start chirruping. A couple plonk down onto their bottoms. From the corner of the room, Archie cranes his little head around from Miss Hubbins' legs. He looks straight at me, then raises his arms up to his teacher to get picked up. He clings on like a monkey, sucking his thumb wide-eyed, watching the show.

I'd rehearsed the next bit. How I would rescue the children. Walking out onto the schoolyard with kids behind me like the pied piper. The applause. An interview for the local paper.

Archie's arms are wrapped around his teacher. He still sleeps in Mum's bed. She says he can't bear to be without her. She has a way of mixing up her own needs with ours. A couple of weeks ago, she slapped my face and locked herself in the bathroom when I called him Oedipus. I was more shocked by the fact she got the reference than the sting of her hand. On that night, I imagined him wetting himself from fear of the gun before I rescued him; Mum wringing her hands and bathing in self-blame on the playground before I step out, reminding her she has two children. She runs to us, relieved. Holds me tight like we're sisters.

I start my speech to Jake.

'Jake, I know you've got lots of big feelings right now, but...'

Hammering at the door interrupts me. The sirens are real.

'Jake, why don't we...'

He's not listening, jumping at each bash against the door. As he swings between looking at me then the door, the gun cuts through the air and the teachers pull the kids back, leaning over to cover more tiny torsos.

Jake's lip is wobbling, so his words come out in a stutter.

'I can't see him, Christie,' he says, looking like he might cry. Like he needs his mum.

Jesus, don't speak to me, don't mention Archie. I stare so hard it aches my eyes. Shut up, for God's sake.

'It's alright, Jake, it's just Mr Sparks talking through the door. Why don't you point that gun down at the floor? I know you don't really want it to go off. Just point it down.'

'Christie, I can't see the kids, they all look the same, I can't find...'

I need to act before he names my brother. Or something worse that I never wanted. Did I? The sirens are getting nearer. I raise my tied hands in the air and run towards him. I want to show him I'm still tied up, show I'm no threat, but my run is all wobbly as my legs aren't working right, and I just fall into him. The main doors are starting to push against the slide, moving it inch by inch. They will be in here soon.

Archie shouts over from his teacher's arm.

'Don't hurt my sister!' The whole world slows down. Jake lifts his head and gun as he clocks Archie. I hear screaming but don't know if it's me or the teachers. As if we're underwater, sounds muffle, and my movements are too slow, too slow. I unhook my hands out of the belt that was never tightened and grab for the shotgun. To my right are the glass doors out onto the play area. That's the way they will come for us. I try to form the words 'fire escape' into Jake's ear, but he doesn't look like Jake anymore, and he rams the butt of the gun into my shoulder and knocks me to the floor.

Archie wriggles out of Miss Hubbins' arms and runs towards me, arms out like he could pick me up and carry me away. All the wrong way around. From down here, his freckled nose and thick strawberry-blonde hair remind me of a picture of myself that I tore into pieces. My scowling face in a holy communion dress, not wanting to look like a mini-bride waiting to have her heart broken. Archie lands on top of me and clutches at my body. I become the new monkey mother. One of those wire ones in experiments that electrocutes the monkey babies, but they cling on all the same as it's better than having no mother at all.

Jake lowers the gun so it hangs as loose as his face. He's making a gurgling sound in the back of his throat like a curlew. I pull myself up with my brother wrapped around me. Jake's frowning in concentration, his body swaying a little bit. He shakes his head slowly, not knowing what to do. Not knowing what I want him to do.

'It's okay, Jake, we're going to leave out of the fire door now. Just drop the gun on the floor and come with us.'

Jake mumbles like he's reading to himself from a script. 'Ignore anything I say, ignore it.' I remember saying that and meaning it. My body turns cold like I need layers and layers wrapped around it after being dragged out of the sea. From the corner of my eye, I can see an outline of figures approaching from outside the fire doors.

The doors crash open, and adults swarm into the room. Jake raises the shotgun back up. I swing my brother out of harm's way. All at once, there are people running, shouting, movement all around me that blurs into stripes. All I can focus on is Jake's face looking straight past me, then his eyes closing as he pulls the trigger.

A gut-punch. Blood. Eyes and hands over me. I want to cover my ears to stop the high-pitched scream bursting my eardrums, but my arms won't move. My body not my own, jostling about as I'm moved into painful daylight. A man talking into my ear, asking me questions I can't hear while hands press into my chest. A mask over my face pouring oxygen in, taking thoughts out. Four police officers huddle on the floor. I can't see Jake underneath them. Children run across the playground like lambs escaping the sound of a passing train. As they hoist me into the ambulance, I think I catch a glimpse of Archie. The arms that embrace him seem to turn from Miss Hubbins' into my mum's. I watch as if from just above them as she strokes his hair, whispering, *I'm here, I'm here, I love you,* and I see it's now changed to my own face that looks back up at her and says, 'Help me, Mummy.'

The Price of Gingerbread

My brother Hansel went missing. Father frowned into whisky. His wife rubbed kohl down her cheeks before posting selfies on Facebook.

Hansel said he'd spied a shack with walls made from bottles of cherry vodka in the marshlands. He liked to get high on hope. He'd have made a great spaniel, yapping about on the daily walk as if it might be different one time, as if paths weren't already mapped out to always end in the same place.

But a twin is only a twin with a twin.

Through the squelch of mud, I tracked his route. The shack was set back in some trees. Columns of cigarette packets created beams to hold the structure upright. I could have sprinkled those white sticks along the path I'd walked, but what was the point when nobody would search for us? Glass bottles arched across the roof. Leeching out of the place was a scent far heavier than Father's shirts, woody and dark. I sniffed until the sky spun.

Lights blinked around the door in green and red. I dug my fingers into a crevice to ease out a mobile phone but didn't know the passcode.

After that, it's hazy. Hansel and I were back together yet hardly there at all. There were fiery drinks poured straight from the rafters, sherbet to rub on our gums, pastilles that turned day to night. We giggled like the toddlers we'd been before Father's eyes were glazed by grief.

We're not alone here, but let's not spoil the tale. Let's not sour the sweet with flashbacks. None of it matters: the strangers, the pressing, the pain. We have the house, and the house has us.

My brother reaches out to squeeze my hand. Then we turn to the walls and gorge ourselves.

Matter

Gas

Before I married, I was a plume of gas. His hands grasped through me. Slowly, slowly, I set into that which can be held. Or be hurt. My cracked lips taste of summer on the turn. I press on raised veins on the backs of my hands, trace a map of mortality along my skin. Never to return to a noble gas, perhaps I can cling to another to become a compound. What distinguishes a gas from a solid is the vast separation of its particles. Eyes closed, I exhale until I'm empty, until each fragment of me lets go.

Liquid

The bed whimpers as I try to leave her. She bows her mattress and pulls me back in: concave to my convex. I dream of all who lay here before me as she drinks my energy. Another day passes. I hear the stomp of my husband's boots against tiled floors below. He's stopped asking if I feel better. One floor of the house each seems fair. I turn onto my front to face her and sink in. She whispers through my skin, *stay*. I wrap myself in the duvet, melt my organs like caterpillar soup, wait until dawn to decide.

Solid

Words pierce arteries, slash stomachs, cause damage deep inside the brain. But only if you let them in. Solidify. Turn each vowel and consonant to mush against statue skin. Stretch out the sounds to breaking point. Repeat them so there's no end and no beginning. Blow them into the air and see their dandelion beauty as they split and scatter. When your mind wishes to echo those words hurled at you, sweeten them. With your arms wrapped over your gift of a body, repeat only those phrases you would whisper to a child. A cloak of compassion protects you now.

Opposite of a Girl

I felt a warning shot in my guts halfway down the third aisle of the superstore. Before I could grab Dad's hand and find the exit, it was too late. My skin turned translucent. Clothes slid from its slippery surface. I could only stare down at my internal organs. Rows of perfumed toiletries shuddered. Dad pretended not to notice. But I saw his nose wrinkle at the putrid smell. Layers of twisted intestines pulsated along with my heartbeat. The thudding in my ears echoed, get out, get out, get out.

Everyone has organs, the adults said. *It's not so different.* But their eyes wouldn't settle on me, darting anywhere but north. Their insides were covered by skin and cloth. I inhaled their lavender necks and dewberry torsos. My crossed arms twitched with the urge to move like poetry. But their job was only to cover me.

I wrapped myself in thick dark felt. The material held out a few hours before congealing onto my wet innards. 'Who died?' a boy shouted from his bike in the park. I pulled my hat lower, shading huge eyeballs that couldn't be tamed with a blink.

I talked and talked so they would only look at my mouth. Rivers of words flooded the room, leaving no space for questions or close inspection.

My skin started to regrow, coarse and dry. I shut my bedroom door.

It started with buds. I plucked them out and threw them on the compost. But in that early morning silence, I ran my fingers over bending bristles of grass on my abdomen and exhaled. A lawn of my own. I folded the black felt suit and tucked it away at the back of the wardrobe. I refused school and turned my torso to the sun. I dozed with my eyes half-open to immerse myself in healing green. Tiny trumpets of colour unfurled and sang to bees and butterflies.

I became beautiful.

That earthy smell followed me. But the creatures knew it takes earth and rot to create life.

ACKNOWLEDGEMENTS

The author and publisher wish to thank the editors of the publications in which the following stories first appeared, online or in print:

'Rules of the High Wire' first appeared in *Flash Frontier*, June 2017; 'Born from Red' – *Bristol Short Story Prize Anthology* Volume 10, October 2017; 'Aspects of My Father' – *Things Left and Found by the Side of the Road* (Bath Flash Fiction Award Anthology), December 2018; 'Waking Beauty' – *Dear Damsels*, June 2017; 'Quads' – *Five2One Sideshow*, June 2018; 'The Fairground' – *Moonpark Review*, June 2018; 'The Science of Self' – *Legerdemain* (National Flash Fiction Day Anthology), July 2021; 'Games O'Clock' – *Bacopa Literary Review*, November 2016; 'A Hunger That Can't Be Undone' – *Ghost Parachute*, June 2018; 'Geology of a Girl' – *Sleep is a Beautiful Colour* (National Flash Fiction Day Anthology), June 2017; 'Stasis' – *Literary Orphans*, October 2018; 'Stop, Stop, Stop, Go' – *Barely Casting a Shadow* (Reflex Fiction Anthology), May 2018; 'The Price of Teeth' – *Flash Fiction Magazine*, August 2017; 'The Accidental CEO' – *Funny Pearls*, December 2018; 'Birthday Present' – *Thief Magazine*, February 2017; 'Davey, Plastic Jesus and the Holy Spirit' – (as 'Swarm') , *Bath Short Story Award Anthology*, December

2021; 'Leftovers' – *Spelk*, October 2017; 'The Never-Quites, Never Quite, Never' – *Cambridge Flash Fiction Prize (TSS)*, July 2020; 'Semaphore' – *The Lobsters Run Free* (Bath Flash Fiction Award Anthology), December 2017; 'Six Decades of Savouring' – *Black Pear Press Short Story Competition Anthology*, November 2016; 'Everything Must Go' – *b(OINK)*, June 2017; 'Dalmatian Readings 1984–1989' – *Cabinet of Heed*, November 2017; 'What to Do When You Can't Do Anything' – *Mechanics Institute anthology*, September 2017; 'Anatomy of a Marriage' – *New Flash Fiction Review*, September 2018; 'Instructions for the Use of Sulphuric Acid for Aesthetic Purposes' – *Storgy*, August 2017; 'See-Through' – *Aesthetica Creative Writing Award anthology*, December 2017; 'The Price of Gingerbread' – *Restore to Factory Settings* (Bath Flash Fiction Award Anthology), November 2020; 'Matter' – as 'Gas, Liquid, Solid', *New Flash Fiction Review*, May 2019; 'Opposite of a Girl' – *Pigeonholes*, May 2017.